Stories 4 Those Of Us
With A Short
Attention Span

Other books by Chris Cooke available at :
www.chriscooke.net

<u>Fiction</u>

THE RIDE

Stories
For Those Of Us
With A Short Attention
Span

This book is dedicated to all my family and friends.
You are all in here somewhere...thanks for the inspiration!

The unaware life, it is said, is not worth living. It cannot even be called life; it is a mechanical, robot existence; a sleep, an unconsciousness, a death. . .

Anthony De Mello

What if what you term as your God heard everything that you thought
and considered that thought a request to give that thing to you...
would you change the way that you think?

Steven Harfield

All the joy the world contains comes through wishing happiness for others. All the misery the world contains comes through wanting pleasure for oneself.

Shantideva

Our present condition is not something causeless nor is it something caused by chance. It is something we ourselves have steadily constructed through our series of past decisions and the actions of body, speech and mind that arose from them.

Dalai Lama

What can a thoughtful man hope for mankind on earth, given the experience of the past million years?

Kurt Vonegut

We are what we repeatedly do.

Aristotle

People *can* come together in spirit and live in peace.
I know they can. . . geez, they have to. . .eventually. . .right?
I have to believe that.

Utopia Boy

CONTENTS

<u>Selected Stories</u>

FORWARD

Ahhhh.....the view from room 2261at Harrah's hotel in Reno, Nevada...overlooking the Truckee river and mountains beyond. Along with my red betta fish named...Reno (I know, I know) and armed with over 10,000 songs on my Zune, 11 candles, my laptop and plenty of Pabst Blue Ribbon beer...I have been having the time of my life writing these short stories! I would listen to music with the candles lit and watch Reno swim around...all while drinking a beer...or two...

I have cherished the many times I rode my bike up the Truckee river until I find a nice spot to stop and write...what an awesome outlet for my soul to run around for a while and dig the opportunity to be creative. I've also been flying 8 different kites at Rancho San Rafael Park which, if you are an adult feeling all the pressures of life...*go fly a kite!* The little kid inside you will thank you...I promise! I must note that I did manage to get my *alien* kite to 1,000 feet on a very good day thank you very much!

I have to mention a weird fact at this point and that is how for the last five years or so, I keep seeing the number 11 everywhere...and I mean everywhere...to the point where it is kinda freaky so I must point out that the numbers of my hotel room do add up to....that's right 11....I just felt it was necessary to point that out..... and I don't know why!

Okay, what have I learned from living in a hotel / casino?

1.) 50/50 is *not* good odds when your whole paycheck is on red.

2.) I had no idea elevators were such a challenge for most people.

3.) You can't walk in a straight line through a casino.....you just can't. The drunks will always thwart and outwit you no matter how sober or focused you are!

Alright, enough of my bagatelle (Yes! I finally used that word in a sentence!) rambling...I really hope you enjoy this book as much as I enjoyed writing it!

The Fortune Cookie

Westminster Abby, Churchill's War bunker, Buckingham Palace, the Globe Theater . . . so far Jack Harper was taking in all the sights and sounds of London, England. He had planned this trip for so long. He had seen all these sights on his first day and still had three weeks to go. As he rode the tube from Saint Paul's Cathedral, he smiled to himself as he thought about where he was going to eat dinner tonight.

Jack had played piano all his life and was a huge Warren Zevon fan. Back in his hometown of Albuquerque, New Mexico he played in a Top 40 band called, "Zero Tolerance." He always got the crowd dancing with his rousing tongue and cheek versions of "Lawyers Guns and Money" and "Werewolves of London" which were both Zevon songs. Now he was speeding through the underground toward Leicester Square and China Town. He found out through an internet search that there really was a Chinese restaurant called, "Lee Ho Fook" and it was the same one that Warren sang about in the werewolves song . . . ever since then he had wanted to try the beef chow mein there.

The tube slowed to a stop and Jack exited into the crowd making his way through the tunnels and escalators to emerge into the hustle and flow of Leicester Square. Weaving his way north he passed by the Venue theater and angled west then North again to enter Chinatown proper and there was Lee Ho Fook's . . . just like in the picture on the internet. Jack marveled at how cool it was that he was really here in London after so many years of dreaming about it.

He walked up to Lee Ho Fook's and right on the big front glass window was a picture of Warren Zevon proudly stating that this was indeed *the* same restaurant that was in the song! Jack laughed to himself and opened the door. Walking into the foyer he was greeted by the hostess who bowed and led him to a table by the window. Jack sat down, ordered some sake and looked out the window at the constant stream of people walking outside.

"People watching" was something that Jack really got into. Looking out at the bustling street, Jack zeroed in on an old Chinese lady bundled against the cold, a silk scarf covering her face. Her clothes were worn however, and one could see upon closer inspection that her scarf was her most decadent luxury. Looking at her face, Jack could see a fierce beauty in her features that was once, long ago, a beauty that would lead a country to war. Now the silk scarf was her metaphor for a beauty that she perceived as gone but was, in reality, ever more present as evidenced by the spark in her eyes.

The waitress returned and handed Jack a menu but he waved her off saying that he would just have the beef chow mein. She bowed and left for the kitchen. Jack was so hungry he felt as if his stomach was turning inside out and eating itself. Taking another sip of sake, Jack stared at a young man who was standing braced against the cold in a leather trench coat, sucking furiously on a cigarette with a faraway stare that could not be penetrated. Jack noticed that at the top of the trench coat he could just make out a black shirt with a white collar underneath . . . a Catholic priest . . . Jack's mind raced trying to decipher this enigma. Was he contemplating his faith? Did he have an affair with a woman and was now in a self created purgatory that tore at both sides of his human condition? Ahhhh . . . Jack pursed a smile . . . the human drama . . . everyone had a

2

fascinating story to tell . . .

"You.. Beef ..a ...chow mein sir." The waitress took Jack by surprise as he pondered the forlorn priest.

"Thank you very much."

Jack watched the steam rise from his chow mein and smelled the flavor as it rose past his nose. Twirling his fork into the noodles, he greedily took a huge bite, burning his tongue with his impatience. "Oowww" he mumbled as he sucked air in and out of his open mouth to try and cool off the noodles only to see a very "proper" English gentleman roll his eyes disapprovingly at his extreme lack of manners.

"Nice..." Jack thought to himself as he sucked the chow mein down. The meal didn't last very long as Jack ate like a junkyard dog who was thrown raw meat over the fence. The waitress took the empty plate and Jack leaned back to unfasten the top button on his jeans until he saw the disapproving stare from the same English gentleman who had busted him before. Feeling as if his stomach would burst through the denim if he didn't, Jack smiled at the man and unbuttoned himself and let out a big sigh and a small burp. The man "hurrummpphed" and continued "properly" mauling his duck. Jack smiled in spite of himself and "Duck man." Reaching onto the table he grabbed the fortune cookie the waitress left in front of him and cracked it in half. Pulling the paper fortune out, Jack shoved one half of the cookie into his mouth and began crunching loudly on it as he held the fortune up to read it.

TONIGHT YOU DIE.

Jack instinctively looked around the restaurant hoping to see one of his buddies laughing at their practical joke........but snapped back to London, England....reality....... and the fact that he was on vacation....alone......

"Musta been a very bad day for the disgruntled worker who wrote this note...." Jack smiled at his fearful reaction and steeled his male ego. Eating the other half of the cookie he saw the waitress look at him from across the room in her attentive way and he beckoned her over.

"Can I have another fortune cookie please?"

The waitress nodded and left to fulfill the request.

Jack looked out the window and saw white flakes of snow dancing in the lights of neon China town. It was a beautiful scene.

"Here. ...fortune ..cookie sir.....may I get.....anything else for sir?"

"No, thank you, just the check please."

As she left, Jack thought how ridiculously paranoid he was being......he stared at this new fortune cookie and hesitated....what if this one.......

"This is stupid....I can't believe I am actually freaked out by this...."

He cracked open the cookie and pulled out the paper.

TONIGHT YOU DIE.....JACK.

Jack froze in his chair and felt his face flush as he tried to wrap his head around the situation.

He looked slowly around the room and every face seemed unfriendly to him as his mind raced.

"You...check..sir."

The waitress handed him the bill and went to the table where "Duck man" had finished and gave him his fortune cookie. Jack didn't know what overcame him but he shot up and before he knew what was happening, he had snatched the cookie from the man, cracked it open and was pulling out the paper fortune as the man said, "I say! Here here man! Have you no couth?"

YOU WILL MAKE A CHANGE FOR THE BETTER.

Jack scowled at the standard fortune he had read at least three times

4

before in various fortune cookies over the years and suddenly realized that "Duck man" had made for the exit. He was mumbling loudly to the waitress as he pulled on his coat and stalked out into the night.

Jack walked quickly toward the waitress.

"I want to see where you keep your fortune cookies please."

"I no...understand..."

"I...want...to....see...where...you....keep...the...fortune....cookies."

Jack was speaking slowly and deliberately to her as if she were a two year old who had hidden the car keys.

"May I help you sir?"

The manager had seen that things were amiss and was now standing between the waitress and Jack.

"Yes, I want to see where you keep the fortune cookies."

"This is vewy strange wequest sir...."

"I know but....look....I'm not crazy....I just.....need to see them if that's OK......*please*...."

Figuring that the best way to diffuse the situation and get this man out of his restaurant, the manager led Jack toward the kitchen.

Pushing open the swinging doors, Jack followed the man to the back and a big shelf that held a huge bag of fortune cookies.

"Here...see this is bag of fowtune cookies...see..."

Jack reached into the bag and pulled out a cookie.

"Pull out a cookie too please." Jack motioned to the manager and the bag.

The manager hesitated but reached into the bag and pulled out a cookie.

"Open it....and read the fortune ....please.."

The manager did as Jack asked and pulled out the paper.

*YOU HAVE A BRIGHT FUTURE AND WILL BE VERY
HAPPY.*

Jack put out his hand and the manager handed him the paper. Jack read it. . .it was as the manager had said.

The manager looked at Jack as if to say, "See, no problem here....stupid American..."

Jack crushed his cookie in his hand and the crumbs fell to the floor as he rolled the paper fortune between his fingers. Taking a deep breath, Jack slowly raised his hand to read it......

*THERE IS NOTHING YOU CAN DO JACK
HARPER...TONIGHT YOU DIE.*

Jack went ice cold and dropped the paper on the floor.

"Are you OK sir?"

Jack just walked slowly out of the kitchen. The manager looked relieved that the situation was winding down.

"This can't be real..........how the.....what the.......why me.." Jack mumbled as he grabbed his coat off the coatrack and made his way through the foyer and out into the waiting night.

The snow fell gently and peacefully in stark contrast to Jacks pounding heart and wild imagination.

"This can't be real......I mean.....I've only been here.....twelve friggin' hours........what the fuck....I have to pull it together....this can't be happening...."

Jack hunkered over as he walked through Chinatown and out onto Charing Cross road. As he went to cross the street, he looked left and started to step out into the street when a flash of red caught his eye and a double decker bus caused him to jump back onto the sidewalk, narrowly missing him as it raced by.

"Look right then left....*right then left*....they drive on the other side of the road.....I'm so stupid!"

6

Jack wondered if he had just cheated the death that the dire cookie had foretold.

"I've only got to walk five blocks.....I can get back alive....surely.....I just have to be really careful...."

Jack's thoughts wandered to ways he could die.....if tonight was indeed the night.....

Robbery gone bad... car....double decker bus (again?) Could it be as simple as dying in his sleep?

Jack was now mumbling relentlessly to himself,

"Geeez.....this is screwed! I have to think positive here........just be careful....pay attention........if it *is* my time, I've had a good life......been a good person......how can a stupid fortune cookie do this? What are the odds that I get three cookies from the same disgruntled fortune cookie writer? It's possible....someone wins the lottery once a week.....those are big bad odds and someone always wins....it's possible......."

Jack continued mumbling and walking until he came to Oxford Street and crossed over to Tottenham Court road. He looked at the huge statue of Freddie Mercury that perched atop the marquee of the Dominion Theater that boasted two sold out years of the show, "*We will rock you*." Jack smiled for the first time since leaving Lee Ho Fook's as he recalled his favorite Queen song, "Fat bottom girls."

Turning onto Adeline place, Jack walked up the stairs to the entrance of his building and looked around as he fiddled for his keys. Turning the key in the lock, Jack pushed open the door. He crossed the entryway and rounded the corner. As he headed down the stairs, Jack saw a stunning brunette bending over in tight sweat pants that said, "honeypot" boldly (and accurately) across her round ass. As she was taking her clothes out of the community dryer, she turned to him and said, "hello" in a French accent. Jack smiled back and

7

managed a nervous "Hi...." On any other normal day Jack would have stopped and talked to her, trying all his best "moves" just to spend one intimate moment with such a beautiful woman. Instead, Jack was already opening the door to his flat and scanning the room for.....death......big surprise, the flat was empty and death was nowhere to be found.....or maybe death was just running late. Jack chuckled to himself and started to relax a little as he turned on the TV and hung up his jacket. He started some water boiling to enjoy a cup of English tea. He had made it back to his flat, and safety.

Jack moved to the window and unfastened the latch. Sliding the window upward, small paint chips floated to the ground as the old window protested the movement like an old man being led away from the pizza slice at the buffet by a doting wife concerned about his cholesterol. The water was now boiling and Jack poured it into the waiting cup. As the tea steeped, he lit a cigarette and leaned on the windowsill overlooking the community courtyard below that was lit by a lone old streetlamp. Blowing smoke gently into the air outside, the chill of the crisp evening air assaulted him but it felt refreshing as he continued to contemplate his strange day. Laying the cigarette in the ashtray on the windowsill, Jack went to his "cuppa" and squeezed out the tea bag. Moving back to the window he picked up the cigarette and sipped at the tea, it was now 10:30 P.M. and he could feel the slow creep of jet lag start to pull at his consciousness.

Jack crushed the smoke out in the ash tray and lit another one to finish his tea with. He started to think about tomorrow and all he things he had planned to do and see. Stonehenge, Salisbury Cathedral and the coup de grace was the London Eye at night to see the lights of London up and down the Thames. His excitement was still buffered by that damn fortune cookie though. Finishing his tea,

8

he took one more puff of the cigarette, crushed it out and closed the window, leaving it open a crack to let some fresh cool air in while he slept.

The bed felt like heaven as Jack realized how tired his legs and back were from all the walking he did today. As he closed his eyes he wondered if he would indeed, die in his sleep. He recalled the Kenny Rodgers song, "The Gambler" and singing, "*the best that you can hope for is to die in your sleep.*"

"Oh well.....if Kenny says so then it must be the best way to go" he thought as he drifted off to sleep.

Jack shot awake as the crash of breaking glass jolted him out of his slumber.

"What the fuck!"

Jack stared into the darkness of his flat as his eyes struggled to gain some foothold against the mountain of blackness that was now pressing against his very soul. He heard a muffled scream and hushed tones coming from outside his window. Quietly making his way across the room to the window, Jack parted the curtains to look upon the dimly lit courtyard below. He saw the hot French laundry chick being held by the throat, suspended in the air by a towering brute of a man who was waving a wicked looking knife in front of her face. She was trembling in his grasp and as he waved the knife by her right eye her whole body went limp anticipating the worst.

Jack was frightened beyond anything he had ever known. He was a simple guy who grew up in the suburbs of Albuquerque and had only been in one fight his whole life and that was in the fourth grade......he had won that fight so technically he was undefeated in his illustrious fighting career. However, this was a far cry from fourth grade and Stevie Nichols' pathetic sissy punches that Jack had so easily deflected.......much to the thrill of the girls on the

9

playground. Now there was another damsel in distress but the stakes were much higher than a caning by the principal.

It was a one story drop to the courtyard below........the man was now holding the point of the knife millimeters in front of the woman's right eye and her face was an awful gray color and her lips were turning blue......if Jack was going to do something.....it had to be now. He reached for the water boiler pitcher and without thinking he threw it through the window which shattered, sending glass hailing down on the struggle blow. In this brief moment of distraction, Jack launched himself out of the window and fell in slow motion right on top of he startled man. Jack saw the woman go flying in one direction and heard the knife skitter and clang off into the darkness. Jack started raining blows to the man's head and face and heard himself yelling, "Fuck you! You son of a bitch! I'll fucking kill you!" Jack had the man on the ground and barely dodged his massive right fist as it whizzed by his head but as he dodged that, the man's left hand came up in the same fluid motion and locked onto Jack's throat. The man was so strong and Jack heard an awful crunching sound emanate from his esophagus.....Jack felt panic set in and shook wildly at the death grip as the man rolled him over on his back. Jack saw the wild, feral look of bloodlust in the eyes of his attacker. The man now sat atop Jack and held his throat tight and Jack realized that he was indeed going to die tonight......he thought that he never would have guessed this was how it was going to end though.

The man looked Jack squarely in the eye and loosened the grip on his throat.

"You stupid shit! She's the devil.......you don't know what a mistake you're maaaaaa........k..i..ng....." He never finished the words as Jack felt a warm liquid spill on his chest and saw the tip of a knife directly in the middle of the man's chest and looked to see the girl standing over the man with a look of hatred in her eyes as she twisted the knife that was impaling the man. Jack heard a terrible crunching sound as the blade scraped bone and shredded organ tissue. Blood was pouring on Jack's face and body and the man's lifeless eyes stared right through Jack's very soul into whatever afterlife only he could see. Jack pushed the man's lifeless corpse off him, rolled over and vomited.

"It's OK now, he can't hurt us anymore....are you all right?" Jack couldn't believe that after this ordeal he was actually embarrassed to have thrown up in front of the hot French chick.

"Yeah....uummm....I guess so..." Jack felt the man's blood start to cool and clot on his skin and clothes.

"Let's get inside and clean you up."

"Sure.....um...shouldn't we call the police or something?" Jack was only now realizing that nobody else was around meaning this whole "incident" was only witnessed by three people and one of them lay dead in a pool of blood. Calling the police was a good idea.....yes...definitely.

"We will as soon as we get you cleaned up and make sure you are OK."

Jack crawled to his feet and felt a wave of nausea rush over him but he kept it down this time and proceeded to follow the woman through the door to the courtyard, up the stairs and into her apartment. As soon as Jack entered, the woman closed the door behind them and Jack turned to her.

"What just happened......"

"Shhhhhh...." the woman put a finger to Jack's lips and pulled him to her and kissed him hard on the lips.

11

"Thank you for saving my life......" she cooed and continued kissing him passionately.

Jack couldn't believe this was happening but was suddenly overcome by the adrenaline that was still coursing through his body from the life and death struggle and swept her into his arms. Carrying her to the couch he threw her down and ripped off his shirt. He lay on top of her and they kissed forcefully as she wrapped her legs around him and began to grind her hips into his. They made angry love and when it was over they lay together in a pool of sweat, semen and dried blood.

"Mmmmm...lover....you American's know how to treat a lady yes...."

Jack looked over at her heaving breasts and wondered what the fuck just happened. Reality came crashing down on him as he finally realized what all had gone on in just the last 30 minutes here.

"We really need to call the police now........geez....I don't even know your name....."

"My name is not important lover.....I will get the phone for you yes." She rose from the couch and sauntered very casually across he room. Jack felt his head start to spin again and realized that his neck was sore and swollen.

"I need a doctor......" he thought.

The woman came back in the room and was brandishing a gun.

"What the fuck is that for..." Jack stammered.

"For you to kill yourself with.....lover...."

Jack though briefly that this might be a joke until he saw the bloodlust in her gaze and his next thought was how to get the hell out of there. As he began to stand, she raised the 9mm pistol.

"You will sit back down now yes."

Jack fell back into the couch.

"There is no better rush than murder and sex no?" she said coyly.
"Look.....whatever it is that you want.....I will do whatever
OK....please don't kill me..."
"But you must die lover....you can identify me to those who
would....how you say....ah yes incarcerate me for my bad deeds."
"Look....I will get on a plane back to the states right now and you
will never have to worry about me identifying you....ever....I
promise!"
"And I should believe you stupid American.....hah.....that is a joke
yes! No, I am sorry....but now you must die."
She raised the gun toward him and gestured toward the balcony.
Jack got up from the couch and slowly began a backwards march to
the balcony, all the while looking at the gun pointed at his chest.
This was unreal......how can this really be happening? Jack hoped
that he would wake up any second in a cold sweat and laugh about
the wild dreams he had and continue his sightseeing of London as
scheduled in his well-laid out itinerary. Glancing at the table by the
balcony, Jack saw a group of newspaper clippings that had been
carefully laid out next to a photo album.
London police baffled by a rash of killings in Bedford square.
Search continues for the "John killer."
Bedford square "John killer" strikes again.
The woman saw him looking at her "collection" and laughed.
"Yes, it is me American. I am the "John killer." A prostitute can
only take so much before she must take back from the men who
continue to behave in such a depraved manor no? These sorry fucks
will never hit another woman again."
Jack was stupefied by this latest revelation. What did he do to
deserve this?
"Sit in that chair on the balcony and open your mouth so this will
look like a suicide yes."

13

She walked toward him bringing the pistol up.

Jack had nothing to lose now. His act of being a good Samaritan had really turned out quite bad and the fortune cookie was right....or was it? He felt a rage well up inside of him as he started to get defiant and wanted to prove that stupid cookie wrong. Before he knew what happened, he lunged toward the woman and heard the gun go off. There was a sharp burning pain in his chest as the bullet went right through his body. Jack realized through the pain that he had his hands around her throat and drove her onto the floor with a crash as the gun fired again missing him. Drywall floated down from the ceiling from the bullets impact as Jack looked into her bulging eyes. The pain was excruciating but still he squeezed as her struggle waned. The gun fell out of her hand and her eyes went cold as she died with a look of surprise on her face. Jack did not let go for a good minute after she took her last gurgling breath. Feeling a wave of dizziness overcome him, he saw that he was bleeding all over the place from his chest wound. He let go and rolled over onto his back on the floor beside the "John killer." It as at this moment that the door burst open in a hail of splintering wood and five policemen rushed into the room guns drawn.

The first policeman to reach Jack was a young man who stared wide eyed at the scene before him.

"My God! Are you OK?"

"I really don't know" was Jack's woozy reply and with that, the room went dark for Jack Harper.

The cacophony of noise woke Jack from his slumber and he opened his eyes to hundreds of people, camera flashes and general chaos as he lay on a stretcher with his chest bandaged and a paramedic standing over him smiling.

"You're fortunate the bullet went right through, we managed to stop

14

the bleeding. You are one lucky man."

"What time is it?" Jack had to know if it was after midnight and he had defied the cookie.

The paramedic looked surprised at this unusual request as he looked at the glowing numbers on his digital watch.

"11:57 PM . . . why? "

"Just had to know is all." Jack smiled despite the pain that wracked his whole body . . . he was going to make it after all.

It was at this moment that the ground began to shake violently.

"What now.......?" Jack mumbled.

The shaking grew worse as bricks and shattering glass from the surrounding buildings came raining down onto the streets below. People were running around wildly and screaming as the ground began to split open all around as entire buildings began to topple over.

Jack lay in his Gurney....vibrating and rolling around the street in the chaos and began to laugh.

"Touche . . . Mr. Fortune Cookie."

Those were the last words that Jack Harper ever said as the earth's magnetic poles shifted and it began to wobble on its axis sending it careening out of its orbit and hurtling through space.

Somewhere in a neighboring galaxy a young sentient life form made a wish on a falling star.

The Poker Game

I don't care anymore . . . no really, I've given up. I am so tired of bad people getting all the breaks. Ya know what I mean? How many times have you seen the backstabbing prick at work get the promotion ahead of you through ass kissing and mediocrity? Let's not even talk about Ashlee Simpson! I know what you would tell yourself cuz I did it too.....*you* tell yourself that although *you* deserved that promotion it was gonna be on *your* terms which have always been, hard work, honesty and loyalty and just in general being an all around good person . . . no backstabbing and debauchery for you right? "The first shall be last and the last shall be first" right? Or how about this oldie but goodie, "Good things come to those who wait." Or my personal favorite, "Do unto others as you wish done to you." WHAT A LOOAAD OF CRAP! And I know what I'm talking about too, I've got the scars to prove it . . . hell, I lived every day of my life by these proverbs and other self help malarkey and look where it's gotten me . . . nowhere that's where!

I was two beers into my ritualistic evening rant when there was a flash of light in my living room and there stood Jesus.
Did you catch that?
I'm talkin' about Jesus friggin' Christ man! The head cheese! The big enchilada! <u>THE</u> *GOD* FATHER......in my living room! Needless to say I was completely speechless.............I just stared wide eyed at him. Jesus smiled the most gentle smile and looked me right in the eyes......as his mouth started to open to speak to me, tears welled up in my eyes and I was ready to hear the most profound, loving, and

16

angelic words issue forth....and he said. ..

"You should tip your beer up. It's spilling on your crotch and looks like you peed your pants."

I dropped the beer on the ground and fell to my knees and began apologizing for the sin of drinking alcohol and between my hands that were clasped in praise appeared an ice cold beer and Jesus said, "Don't drop this one, I hate to see a good beer go to waste."

"That's a pretty cool trick" I said as Jesus helped me to my feet.

"Yeah gets me lots of chicks at frat parties."

I was stunned.

"YOU go to frat parties Jesus?"

"No, but I do have a sense of humor."

We both sat down at my kitchen table and I asked him, "Why are you here to see me? ....am I dead?"

He looked me square in the eyes and said, "No my son, I am here because I am tired of all your bitching and complaining."

I stared down at the table in shame.

Don't be ashamed of that, everyone does it. Every second of every hour of every day.....twenty-four seven, it never stops. Nobody is happy.....ever.....trust me, I know! I have to listen to it constantly."

"Why me?" I said.

"Why not." Was the response.

Jesus raised his arms and said, "Here's what we're gonna do." Suddenly, my kitchen table turned into a beautiful poker table complete with Martini's and lit cigars in golden ashtrays! The deck of cards seemed to float just above the emerald green felt of the table.

Jesus said, "I know you like poker so we are gonna play some heads up Texas Hold Em. We each start with 1,000 in chips and the blinds are 25 and 50. We play no-limit until one or the other is out of chips.

17

If you win, I grant you one answered prayer right here, right now.
If I win, you have to promise to stop your bitchin......Deal?"
I couldn't believe what I was hearing.....this had to be a dream or
something.
"This is no dream" said Jesus.
I looked across the table and said, "You know all my thoughts, how
can we play poker....I mean..... you know everything that has been, is
right now and ever will be."
Jesus laughed and said, "Are you saying I'll cheat!"
I straightened up and stammered, "No, No your holiness I...I.....I...."
Jesus laughed deeply saying he would not use his "powers" and that
it would be a fair game and to just call him Jesus. So I agreed.

    We went back and forth, hand for hand, drinking our Martini's,
laughing and smoking our cigars. I even bluffed Jesus out of four big
pots! I think he was bluffing a couple of times too but when the Lord
moves all-in, it's a little more intimidating than the grizzled old
poker pro who blew in with the desert wind that always scared me at
the poker table. I felt so comfortable as we played and talked and
laughed. He was like the best friend you had known all your life who
you could tell anything to and not be judged by....but was never
afraid to tell you the straight story....even if it meant hurt feelings.
I took a puff of my cigar and looked at my two hole cards that I had
just been dealt. I had a 7, 8 of hearts. I loved playing suited
connectors so I called the big blind. Jesus checked and the flop was
dealt. The three cards hit the table.....9, Queen, 10 ....all hearts.
I had flopped a flush and had a gutshot to the straight flush. I bet
$100 and Jesus called. The turn card was a King of spades. I bet
$100 and Jesus raised me to $200. I called the raise. At this point, I
was putting Jesus on a higher flush or a pair of Kings. The river card
was the Jack of hearts. I had hit my straight flush but if Jesus had the

King of hearts he would have the higher end of the straight flush.......the odds of that were pretty low.....then again this is Jesus we're talking about here. Well, I had to go for it so I moved all-in. Jesus seemed to look right through me and said, "You had a few more chips than me when we started this hand, if I call and lose, I'll be out."
I stared at the table trying my best poker face when he said, "I call."
I flipped over my cards and said, "Straight flush to the Queen!"
Jesus let out a sigh and said, "Beats me" but did not flip over his cards.
I couldn't believe it, I had won...............I looked at Jesus and said, "I'm not gonna go to hell for beating you am I?"
Jesus laughed and said, "Don't be silly now, you won fair and square. I believe that you have a prayer that needs answering so what will it be?"
Wow.
I wanted to make it good..... you know... like something that could really help out myself and others.....heck maybe even the whole planet...................
I looked at Jesus and said, "I want everything to be cool for every living creature on this planet!" I was real proud of that, I believe I had covered everything with that one request.
Jesus said, "Define cool."
I was startled saying, "you know, cool.............. everyone is happy and fulfilled and gets along."
Jesus then said, "Well, your definition of "cool" is not necessarily another person's definition of "cool" so are you asking me to take away free will and bend everyone's will toward your idea of Nirvana"
"Whoa, whoa Jesus" I said ...."I don't want to be responsible for that. How about no more disease."

19

Jesus said, "Then the planet would be horribly overpopulated, do you think that will be paradise?"

"OK, OK what about everyone being fulfilled all the time in their life."

"But isn't that stagnation?" asked Jesus.

He continued, "If people don't have the desire to fulfill a dream or goal, do you think you would have gone to the moon or accomplished all the wonderful art, music, architecture, and philosophical ideas you have now?"

"Yeah Jesus, but what about people whose dream is to kill other people and are pure evil? I mean, that works both ways you know. Maybe I should just wish for no more bad people."

Jesus said, "Even a symphonic piece of music has some minor chords to offset the happier major chords to create tension and release and make the happy chords that much more joyful within the song. Sometimes you need the bad to see the good and be that much more happy and thankful for the good times."

I felt pretty overwhelmed and hopeless so I took a hit from the cigar, sipped my Martini and then it hit me like a gentle wave washing over my soul.

"I want love to be eternal and conquer all."

Jesus smiled and with a glint in his eye said, "It already does."

I sipped the Martini and said, "Can I have a box or two of these cigars and keep this poker table?"

Jesus said, "Sure my son."

Jesus stood up to leave and I asked him, "Hey, am I gonna do something really special with my life?"

Jesus hugged me and said, "You do something special with every breath you take..... maybe your purpose in this life is to have a child who has a child who is going to solve all the world's ills. That's a pretty special purpose in the bigger picture wouldn't you say?"

And with that he was gone.

I sat back down at the poker table and sipped on the Martini and finished off the cigar when I noticed that I never saw the two cards Jesus had in the hand that lost him the game. I flipped over the first card which was a seven of clubs and then the second card......it was the King of hearts.

Amanda

I love Halloween. The seasons are changing, the air is crisp. The leaves on the trees become a myriad of iridescent color that is as intense as a firework at the point of first explosion when the sparks and colors are at their hottest. Now I'm not what you would call the best looking man in the world so I can truly appreciate beauty like this. You see, I worked my whole life in the circus.......I was a...well.....how do you say......oh I'll just come out and say it.......I was a freak. That word always used to bother me until I joined up with my carnival brothers and sisters. They were the first people I had ever met that never chided me or looked away as I walked by. After about a year with them I began to be proud of the fact that I was a freak and the word itself became a source of great power for me. I had thirty-two great and magical years traveling in the side show. I retired about two years ago and had enough money to buy a small house in a nice suburb here in Santa Fe, New Mexico.

I fell in love with the southwest when I traveled there for the first time with the sideshow. There is something magical about Santa Fe that cannot be put into words. You have to experience it for yourself and......well it's probably not for everyone but I am grateful for that as it wouldn't be as nice with lots of people around. Anyway, it's October 31st.....and I had bought a lot of candy in anticipation of the kids in their costumes going door to door around the neighborhood in the traditional showing off of the scariest and most original costumes. As I looked out my window, the twilight was slowly beating down the brilliant autumn sunset and I thought what a perfect night for the children........you see....this was the first Halloween I decided to be a part of since I bought my house. The last two years I sat inside with the lights off as I was not comfortable showing my face to "regular" looking people. Let me tell you, when you are the only house that doesn't pass out treats....you get pretty good at cleaning egg off the windows!

Since I have lived here, I never went outside without a scarf wrapped around my face so as to not upset my neighbors. They were all very friendly but I knew that if they saw me in all my freakish glory, the stares and grabbing of kids as I passed by would soon begin.......Anyway, I had an epiphany earlier this year when I realized that Halloween was the perfect time for me as I could be myself and people would just think I was in a scary mask and costume. Once I realized this I couldn't wait to be a part of the one holiday where I could truly be myself.

Suddenly the doorbell rang! I jumped out of my easy chair and made for the door. My bowl of candy sat on the shelf eagerly awaiting its destiny as a dentist's best friend! I bought the best candy too, they would talk about my wares for the rest of the year! I opened the door and three children sang out in unison, "Trick or treat!"

Their costumes were magnificent! One was Dracula complete with blood dripping down his chin and the little girl was the scariest witch I had ever seen! The other looked just like Agent Mulder from the X-Files. It was quite a spiffy suit I may add! They all accepted their candy graciously and Dracula said, "Nice costume mister!"

I just smiled as they turned and continued their twilight journey. As I started to close the door another group of kids started up my walkway. I heard them saying that I had king size Kit Kat bars. They musta ran into Dracula and his gang. I smiled as I filled their bags with the sweet bounty. This group wore those cheesy store-bought costumes and one boy's glasses were fogged up as he wore them outside the stuffy mask. There was Kenny from South park, Darth Vader from Star Wars and Spider Man.

I passed out candy for a solid two hours when it started to slow down. All that remained were the echoes of happy hoots and hollers around the neighborhood as the kids were probably dealing with the inevitable sugar rush that will make tomorrow's school day full of candy hangovers. I was sitting in my recliner watching "The Great Pumpkin Charlie Brown" feeling very happy that I could have normal interaction with other people......even if it is only one day a year. Yup, tonight I felt more like the confident Snoopy than the ostracized Charlie Brown. Then came a soft knock at the door. I thought all the trick or treating was over for the night but I rose from my chair, glad to make another child happy. I opened the door and there stood a lone little girl in what I think was a fairy princess costume. It was obviously homemade and I noticed that her wand was sagging and the tinfoil star was bent. She said nothing.......just looked at me with big brown eyes.....it reminded me of a deers eyes the way they held wisdom, intent and sadness all in their almond-shaped prison. I noticed that she kept one arm behind her back as she stood there, holding the wand and her candy bag in the other.

"Don't you look pretty." I said with a gentle smile.

"Thank you she mumbled.....you look very scary too sir....."

She averted her eyes as if she was ashamed of what she had said....it was as if she knew that this was the real me and saw right through my Halloween ruse.

"Would you like some candy?" I asked.

"Yes please.." She answered.

She raised one hand toward me and continued to hold the other behind her back. As I poured the candy by the fistful into the bag it suddenly dropped to the ground and candy flew everywhere as the bag split open upon impact. She quickly fell to her knees dropping her wand and started picking up the candy with one hand and wiping tears from her eyes with the other.........well....that was when I noticed that she had no hand but her arm just ended at the wrist. She saw me looking and quickly dropped the candy and turned away walking off quickly with her shoulders moving up and down as she sobbed. Well, I was dumbstruck and shouted out to her, "What about your candy?"

She kept walking away.

"I'll give you another bag to carry it! Please come back!"

She stopped walking but did not turn around.

"Here see, I'll be right back with a bag for you."

I ran to my kitchen and returned to the door. She stood there wiping the tears from her eyes with her good hand and the other was hidden once again. I started to pick up all the spilled candy and she remained silent. I still don't know why I said this but it just came out.

"Did you know that people with your special gift get special candy?" She looked quizzically at me.

"That's right.....usually they show me their gift right away so that I know they are one of the special people."

"What do you mean special?" She asked.

"Why all the people with only one hand" I said.

She turned away in shame.

"You mean that nobody told you how special you are to have only one hand? Well let me show you then!"

I asked her to come into my entryway but left the door open so no one would think that I was up to no good and ran to get the old cotton candy machine I took with me when I left the circus. Cotton candy was my favorite and all the other freaks chipped in to give it to me as a retirement present. I wheeled the machine into the entryway, plugged it in and ran to get the ingredients.

"Hang on princess, I won't be but a second!"

I came back and turned the machine on and poured the ingredients in and asked her to step up to the machine.

"Do you like cotton candy princess?" I asked.

"My name is Amanda but sometimes people call me Mandy and..... yeah..... I *looove* cotton candy."

"Well step right up and wave your arm in the machine but only reach in this far OK."

She reached up with her good hand and I told her that she had to use the other one as that was the only way that the cotton candy would work. She sheepishly raised her other hand and looked at me.

"You wouldn't lie to me would you mister?"

"Of course not Mandy."

She looked me right in the eye and asked me, "Are you wearing a mask?"

I froze where I stood. Her eyes were locked into my soul.

"No Mandy, I'm not.....this is my real face."

She smiled and said OK and reached into the machine and said, "now what?"

I was stunned.....she seemed more at ease with me and was certainly not scared.

"Swirl your arm around....there you go....just like that!"

The cotton candy began to stick to her arm and form it's bulbous shape. She started to laugh and said, "This is fun!"

I was so pleased......she was radiating joy.....this was not the same girl that rang my doorbell minutes ago.

"OK that's enough."

She now had a perfect pink cotton candy treat on her arm and looked at me expectantly.

"Well chow down!" I said.

She looked at me and mumbled, "Did other kids make fun of you too...."

"Yes Mandy they did....."

"What did you do about it?" She asked between bites of the sweet treat.

"Well.......I joined the circus when I was old enough."

She looked past me and said, "So you ran away then......that's what I want to do too."

"Running away isn't the answer Mandy, why would you want to do that?"

"The other kids make fun of me and I don't fit in."

"Well they don't know how special you are now do they."

"WOW! Cotton candy! Can we have some mister?"

It was a late group of trick or treaters. Within seconds, Wonder Woman, Freddie Kruger and another Spider Man stood in my doorway.

"Hey look it's Handy!" Wonder Woman said.

"You mean Nohanda!" Freddie yelled.

They all laughed and Mandy looked toward the ground and her arm with the cotton candy quickly went behind her back. I was so mad......these were obviously some of the kids responsible for Mandy wanting to run away.

"Can we have cotton candy too mister?"

I took a step forward and said, "Do any of you have the gift?"

They looked at each other and Spider Man said, "The gift....what are you talking about sir?"

"You know, the gift....one hand.....oh..... I see you three are all two handers. Well no cotton candy for two handers but I do have other candy for you."

"But we want cotton candy!" They cried.

"Sorry that's just the way it is."

"But that's not fair." Pleaded Freddie Kruger.

"Maybe so but that's the way it is....now do you want candy or not?"

"You suck" said Spidey.

"C'mon let's go!" Yelled Freddie.

"Hey mister, your mask sucks too!" Chided Wonder Woman.

I knew that I would be cleaning egg off the window in the morning but I was glad to put them in their place. I turned to Amanda and she still had her hand behind her back. I looked her in the eye and told her that she was special and to never let anyone tell her differently because she was destined for great things in life and to never give up.....*ever*.

"You better eat your cotton candy Mandy" I said.

She pulled her arm around and started in on the treat."Mmmm. . . it's good" She said between mouthfuls. She was smiling again.

"You best get home before your parents worry."

"Thanks sir."

"Call me Ben OK Mandy."

"Bye Ben....thanks."

She turned and walked away. I watched her as she disappeared down the street tearing pieces off the cotton candy as she walked. I closed my door and turned the cotton candy machine off. I sat back down in my chair and that's when I heard the *Pap pap pap* of eggs hitting my window. I knew who it was but I didn't care. I had made someone happy tonight and feel special and she didn't even care that I was a disfigured freak. I fell asleep to that thought.

I awoke to the sunlight and a squeaking sound....I had fallen asleep in my recliner by the fireplace. I rubbed the sleep from my eyes and looked at my front window. Amanda smiled a big smile and waved as she cleaned the egg off the window. I went outside.

"Good morning Ben! I knew this would happen so I thought I would help you out. See, I can do the cotton candy with my special arm and clean the window with this one!"

She held up both arms proudly and stood up to face me.

"I will never be ashamed of who I am again.....thanks Ben."

"So no more running away huh?"

"Nope! You know what I'm gonna do Ben?"

"No, what?"

"I'm gonna clean windows until I have enough money to buy an easel and paint and then I am going to be a famous painter!"

"Well that sounds just fine Mandy. How much for my window?"

"This is for free but next time I gotta charge ya....but you will *always* get a discount Ben!"

I'll be damned if Amanda didn't become the premier window washer in the neighborhood. She always gave me a discount and she showed me her brand-new easel and paint set when she bought it. Her art progressed quickly and she always shared it with me....I was so proud.

The years rolled by and Mandy always got cotton candy on Halloween.....and other days of the year cuz I'm a big softy. All too soon it was time for her to leave and pursue her dreams.

Well.....it's been about 10 years now since she left for New York and the big shot art school that she got a scholarship to. She used to write often but I haven't heard much in the last three years or so.....that's OK cuz I just know she is doing well and very happy. It's funny how one moment in time....one brief encounter can change your life or someone else's for the better.......or worse......fortunately

I was happy with the way I handled myself in this life......

One Sunday morning I awoke to the doorbell. I stood up, grabbed my scarf and wrapped my face. I opened the door there stood Amanda! Next to her stood a small girl about three years old and a man who I assumed to be her boyfriend or husband. Mandy grabbed the scarf and before I could do anything, she had pulled off the covering and my disfigured face was exposed.........neither the girl nor the man looked away at the sight of my face......in fact they both smiled warmly.

"Hi Ben! I told you I wouldn't let you wear that damn scarf around me!"

She threw her arms around me and hugged me tightly. She stepped back and proceeded to introduce me to her husband, John and daughter Cynthia. We talked about old times and she apologized for not keeping in touch better. I told her I understood and was very happy and proud of her accomplishments.

"I have a surprise for you Ben....it's a painting I did....it's my favorite ever.....I want you to have it!"

Her husband went out to their car and returned with a picture wrapped in brown canvas. He handed it to Mandy and she pulled back the canvas to reveal a painting of a small child dressed like a shabby princess and a stunningly handsome man in a prince's outfit. It was set in the marketplace of a great castle and they were standing in front of a wooden cart that said **Cotton Candy** in calligraphy style writing. The prince was handing the child some cotton candy and she was beaming with anticipation. The sky was a stunning blue and sunbeams made their way into the courtyard and fell upon the prince and princess.

"Wow, that's beautiful Mandy........I figure that the princess is you and I know you love cotton candy but what's with the prince?"

"Why that's you silly."

"Me.......oh......but he is handsome and.....perfect........and beautiful....."

She hugged me and said quietly, "As are you Ben.....you are the most beautiful person I have ever known.......thank you for giving me life........"

That picture still hangs above my fireplace and I look at with love and fondness every single day. I'd be lying if I said it didn't bring a tear to my eye every single day. Amanda still keeps in touch every now and then but life goes on you know. I always wished that I could be someone who could change lives by being a dashing super hero or a handsome actor but you know what, I changed one life for the better and taught tolerance and acceptance ......you know what....that's enough. If we all did that......... there would be no need for a freak show.

JOHN SMITH GETS A NEW JOB

John Smith never saw the bus coming as he stepped out into the busy street in the pouring rain. The impact threw him 78 feet in the air and his broken body landed in a dumpster behind a sushi bar . . . John hated sushi . . . especially the smell.

According to the coroner, it was a perfect "three pointer" by the bus.....this drew a huge laugh from the menagerie of police, EMT's and other emergency workers. The irony was that John was killed by the number 17 bus . . . the same bus that he took down Broadway to his job every day for the last three years.

Finally able to buy his own car after his girlfriend left him sexually, emotionally and financially bankrupt, this daily hike on the bus with the thralls of people, pushing and pickpockets came to a glorious end when he drove the 1979 Pontiac Firebird he always dreamed about off the used car lot....knowing in his heart that his life was changing for the better. This was only two days ago and today his dream car left him stranded on the parkway bridge...in the rain...after the right rear tire just decided to fall off.

After calling the car lot on his cel phone and finding out that if he would have read his contract, the cvc joint that held the rod, that held the bolt, that held the rod, that held the tire to the axle was not covered under the warranty. The salesman was really sorry and referred John to an, "honest as the day is long" mechanic downtown who could fix the car at a "fair price." Before John could yell at the salesman, he heard his phone beep twice and the battery died. After some choice words, repeated banging on the ceiling of his car, and constantly mumbling, "life sucks....it's just not fair...." John began the mile walk to the towing company he knew resided on 5th and elm. As soon as he exited his car, the rain started coming down even harder and the wind switched direction to now blow the rain horizontally into his face as he trudged on.

"Life sucks.......it's just not fair....."

Walking through the front door of, *Joe's towing and repair*, there was not a dry spot on John's body. He was even soaked where the sun don't shine after a car got too close to the curb and splashed muddy water right up John's crotch.

After an hour in Joe's waiting room with the black and white TV that only tuned in one station, John was waved outside to the waiting tow truck. He frowned as the truck arrived just before they were going to reveal whether or not these beautiful women were really women at all....or really men.....ahhhh....another intriguing hour with Maury.

To say that the tow truck driver was surly was like saying that a tarantula was cute and cuddly. "Fuckin' rain.....we are fuckin' swamped today with another batch of idiots that go too fast through the water and get the distributer cap wet.......idiots! Today was supposed to be the first day of my vacation and fuck me! Here I am........shit! Fuckin' Murphy! That Motherfucker is relentless......one day he will leave me alone.....he has to...right? What's your story pal?"

"Tire fell off on my car that I just bought two days ago."

The tow truck driver was silent after that as John trumped his story with his own. Apparently Murphy liked....or hated John just a little bit more than the tow truck driver.

"Turn right here, my car is just down this........shit." John looked through the flailing windshield wipers of the tow truck to see his car

33

up on blocks and all four tires were gone.

"Who the fuck steals tires in the fucking rain!" John screamed at the tow truck driver.

The driver just looked solemnly at John and after the pause said, "We are gonna have to send a flatbed for your car, I can't tow it like that on the boom....sorry man....."

"I have to get to work.......I couldn't call to let them know cuz my cel phone died......can I use yours?" John looked at the driver.

"Sorry pal......I forgot mine at home today and our radio is only two way......"

"Can I get a ride uptown?" John was pleading.

"No can do buddy, I'm going the other way, this is the last stop."

John stood in the rain and watched the towtruck drive away into the mist and moisture.

"Life sucks....it's just not fair...."

Bowing is head to the rain, John began the 5-mile trek to his office. Two blocks from his office, John stepped off the curb to cross Broadway, not noticing the light as it turned red......

"Life sucks....it's just not fair...."

BAM!!!!!!

Now John floated above the scene of his own grisly demise watching as another paramedic made a sick joke at his expense.

"Wow.........I...I....I'm dead......" John held his hand up to his face and saw the scene below right through his now translucent hand. As he stared, he began to rise into the air and the accident below faded into a city block, then the entire city. Soon the earth was racing away from him as he shot through the galaxy and the stars became a blur as he continued his astral journey.

Darkness.

Silence.

Beautiful green meadow.

34

John was in a beautiful meadow looking at a small balding man with thick rimmed glasses. The man wore paisley converse tennis shoes, blue tights with a big red and yellow **M** on the front and finished off the ensemble with a flowing red cape. He looked exactly like superman.....if superman was Mr. Magoo.

"Not what you were expecting eh?"

John was dumbstruck but chuckled in spite of himself and the vision in front of him.

"Are you uh....ummm....God?"

"No, no....I'm Murphy!" The man did a little dance step and fell down on one knee with his arms stretched out before him like he just finished a big number and was waiting for the roar of applause from the audience. "TA DA!"

John stared on in disbelief.

"Wow, I would've thought you would be more impressed....after all, I am the one responsible for all the stupid little aggravating bullshit that you put up with for the last 33 years. I especially liked the stolen tires in the rain today! God I'm good!"

"What are you talking about?" John was incredulous.

"Ah c'mon John, I'm Murphy.....ya know, as in *Murphy's law* Murphy."

"What?" John was feeling woozy at this turn of events and wondered how he could feel woozy when he was dead.

"I'm the one who's responsible for all the event's that happened to you today.....well...except for you dying....that was the big guy did that. Anyway, how'd ya like the ride up here? Pretty cool huh! That was my favorite part of dying ya know. The earth and stars and stuff. Like, cosmic dude!"

"Am I in heaven....umm....Mr. Murphy?"

"Look kid, just Murphy will do OK. And yes...you are in heaven.

God will be around shortly to say "Hi" and give you the tour. I'm here because you're the one pal! I just couldn't wait to greet you and start showing you the ropes and stuff."

"What ropes? What stuff?"

"You're taking my job John. You are going to be the new Murphy!"

"What are you talking about? The new Murphy? What kinda punishment is that?"

"Easy there Johnny boy.....or should I say....Murphy. It's not a punishment at all...in fact, it's one of the best gigs here in heaven! Right up there with being in the band!"

"Band??" John was woozy again.

"Oh yeah, you should hear the band up here! Lennon, Hendrix, Morrison, Holly, Elvis, Stevie Ray....they're all here man! You ain't heard a drum solo 'till you've heard John Bonham and Buddy Rich go at it! Totally rad man!"

John couldn't believe he just heard Murphy utter the phrase "totally rad man."

"C'mon John, let's take a walk. You ain't gonna believe the shit you get to pull on people now! You got any friends that you wanna mess with first?"

And with that, John and the man in the cape walked off through the meadow.

Rosie The Riveter

"Corporations man....that's what's ruining this country."
Will spoke the words with authority as he and his best friend Liam discussed what was wrong with America and how they would solve all the country's woes if they were in charge.

The two friends volunteered once a week at the *Retirement Castle* on Indian School Road in Albuquerque, New Mexico. Since they were both college students who knew everything and wondered what would possess their parents to vote Republican, it was no wonder that the residents of the *Retirement Castle* avoided them...even though most were starved for attention. Apparently, Will and Liam believed that they were going to solve all the planets tribulations when millennia of scholars and research had come up short.

"No, it's because of greed and our amazing system that is designed to sell dignity to the highest bidder...I mean look at how the middle class is disappearing dude! Everyone is all 'me, me, me!' these days and doesn't look at the big picture and how we are all like...one planet and we have to make this work...ya know?"
"But that's caused by the corporations!" Will was still on point.
"No, corporations are just a symptom of a bigger problem. It's all about the battle between spirituality and the super ego...quantum physics is proving that everyday."
"Dude, you are such a hippie."
"Takes one to know one Will."
"I think you're both idiots!"

Old man Mc Cready had wheeled up to the pair unnoticed.

"I can't take it anymore! I......we.... *all of us* have to listen to you two morons discuss the same bullshit every week when you come here! And it is **bullshit**...let me assure you!"

Will and Liam were surprised by the old man's sudden appearance and stood dumbfounded as Mr. Mc Cready glared up at them from his wheelchair.

"Bahhh.....you two aren't worth the effort!"

With that, Mr. Mc Cready deftly spun his wheelchair around and began to head back out of the rec room.

"I suppose you know something we don't there Mr. Mc Cready...I mean...do *enlighten* us... please..."

Will soaked his words in heavy sarcasm.

Mr. Mc Cready raised his arms toward the ceiling and tilted his head back.

"Dear God, if you could answer one more prayer from an old codger, I would appreciate it if you could just make sure that these two dolts have kids that are... *just... like... them*!"

"That's real mature Mr. Mc Cready....real mature." Liam rolled his eyes.

"You're damn straight it's mature ya little punk! I'm 87 years old and I never figured it out.....and I know that I'm a hellova lot smarter than the two of you fruit loops put together!"

"Now that was uncalled for...." Will looked at Liam in dismay.

"No...it is called for! You little punks don't know how good you have it! *Me*...and *my friends* fought and died for you to be able to sit here and have the freedom to have these opinions, ignorant as they are....and I can't help but think, 'I fought for these two'! C'mon, at least use your brain a bit before you open your mouths.....you're young and all wound up about this crap that will never

38

change....when you should be out chasin' skirts! Yup, that's what I was doing at your age! Now it is all too clear why we are graced with your presence every week...how do you fit it into your busy schedule....oh that's right...you don't have dates! Ha ha!"

Mr. Mc Cready was known as one of the crankier tenants at the *Retirement Castle* but he was going for broke today and the other residents had been quietly gathering around the spectacle as "Cranky Cready" (as he was known) let the two boys have it.

"Okay, okay...just hold on here Mr. Mc Cready..."

Liam wanted to end this as peacefully as possible, he had never seen the old guy so animated and wound up.

"You're doing an awful lot of judging and ranting here but if you are 'all knowing' then I really want to hear what you think of all this. Where do you think America got off track?"

"Rosie the riveter." Cranky Cready said the three words with authority.

Will looked at Liam.

"Who's Rosie the riveter?"

Mr. Mc Cready laughed, "I see the brain trust is in good form today! What do they teach you in that college you're going to? I hope you're not paying them for this great education you're receiving!"

Liam addressed Will.

"Rosie the riveter was an iconic figure in World War II that represented the six million women who went to work in the manufacturing plants that produced munitions and material during the war while the men were fighting in the Pacific and European theaters. Dude, you really need to read another book that isn't written by J.R.R. Tolkien or JK Rowling...."

Will turned red and looked around the room which was now silent. He sought a sympathetic glance but found none so he addressed Cranky Cready.

"Alright then...how is this Rosie the riveter responsible for all the chaos in this country?"

Old man Mc Cready wheeled up to them and began to talk. "Before Rosie, there was this thing called a 'family' in this country....worked pretty darn good too! The man worked and the woman took care of the kids. Now before you boys say anything, I'm not advocating the 'barefoot and pregnant' ideal as that is not right either....it's just that the older I get I realize that simplicity works. It just does. The correct solution to any problem is always the simplest. People are what complicate things and muddy the water. Keep that in mind there brain trust."

Will and Liam exchanged exasperated glances.

"Anyway...during the war, all the men were off fighting and we needed bodies in the factories to keep the war effort moving forward and so women stepped in to help out...damn good thing too or we'd all be speaking German right now! But two things happened that I feel answer your question regarding the current state of affairs that you two geniuses are lamenting over. The family unit broke down and the government facilitated it's breakdown. Once women proved themselves as a force in the workplace that could keep up with men, it only took a second for the government to realize that after the war, if they could keep women working, they could quite literally double their taxable income."

The boys looked at each other.

"Ahhhhh I see I struck a chord with the Einstein brothers....." Old man Mc Cready looked very pleased with himself as he continued. "Now it also followed that a family could double their income if both parents worked......what did that leave? I'll tell you what it left, kids to fend for themselves or 'latchkey kids' as they became so endearingly named. Well after a couple generations of this dynamic, is it any surprise that we have the instant gratification, selfish society we have now? With no guidance kids become jaded and full of self purpose only.......do I think women should work? Of course I do...but with the family unit decimated and constantly under duress from ever increasing taxes and mismanaged government...how can we possibly stand a chance when confronted with generations of kids that lack an internal guidance system that is usually instilled from their parents and a stable home.......oh, and these same kids grew up to become the CEO's of these corporations that you so fondly speak of...."

The rec room of the *Retirement Castle* was silent as all eyes focused on Will and Liam and their gaping mouths. Cranky Cready stared at the boys.

"And that boys, is where I think the problem started...put that in your pipe and smoke it..."

Will and Liam just sat, dumbstruck as the residents started to fade back into the nooks and crannies of the *Retirement Castle.*

"Well boys, if you do find a solution to *anything*....do let me know."

Mr. Mc Cready turned his wheelchair around and rolled down the hallway chuckling.

Fear Of The Known

As I opened my eyes and slowly looked around my small studio apartment, I saw dust particles hovering in the sunbeam that sliced through the gap in the curtains......I shuddered thinking how many bacteria swirled in the air that I had to breathe just to live. It wasn't fair that these airborne pathogens were allowed to exist with impunity in the very source of life that I drew in with every breath.

I rose and put on my slippers that I knew were beginning to get ripe with foot fungus or any number of infections that keep a podiatrist's children attending the ivy league schools that are paid for by.........germs!

Shuffling to the bathroom I noticed an ant on the counter and hurriedly reached for the bleach under the sink! After the ant was disposed of and the counter was sufficiently sterilized, I stared at the toothbrush that I knew I would have to put in my mouth......so many germs! Everywhere! My mind raced as I pondered the millions of germs residing in my bathroom........it was overwhelming! Stumbling out of the bathroom, I turned on the TV....I needed a distraction as I gathered the strength to brush my teeth and step into the bacteria stew that was my shower! Just then I heard the reporter on the news chime in with a bone chilling report.....

"*The entire supply of this years flu vaccine has been deemed tainted and unusable by the government health agency....*"

What! I was going to get my flu shot tomorrow! I stared in horror at my television! I knew I shouldn't have waited! Now I would be susceptible to influenza! I turned off the TV and began to shake where I stood........this was bad.....really *really* bad! I looked around my small apartment and felt the germs begin to laugh at my vulnerability! Oh how they mocked me!

Then my doorbell rang! I raced to the door and looked through the peep hole and there stood Mrs. Johnson, the landlady! I was about to open the door when I heard her cough! Oh dear God she's sick! My head swam as I slowly backed away from the door, hoping she had not heard me. As I held my breath it seemed like an eternity until I heard her footsteps receding away from my door and down the hall........Oh what was I gonna do??? I'm trapped in this pathogen-filled apartment!

I ran and washed my hands. . . just because! My head was pounding! I had to get ready for work....I had to go to work but there were so many germs outside! People wanting to shake my hand, second hand smoke, influenza, ebola and sars! Terrorists with dirty bombs, smallpox and animals with rabies and killer bees! The apartment began to spin around me as I realized that I could walk out my door and get crushed as the building collapsed around me as an earthquake shook the city to the ground! What if there was a tornado or hurricane or..or...a....a.... gang doing a drive-by as I walk in the wrong place at the wrong time! I could be abducted by a UFO and probed! The mothman could get me......bigfoot could crush my skull like a melon if he got a hold of me! There was scabies and shingles and herpes and aids and gonorrhea and irritable bowel syndrome and kidney stones and cel phone signals causing tumors in my brain and..... and....ah......ah..ahhhhhhhhhhhhh................

Destinations Unknown

Carl and Wendy sat side by side on top of the old stone arch that was the exit (or entrance, depending on the direction of the train) to the tunnel that went over the railroad tracks near the top of the Tehachapi mountains. Their legs were swinging in unison as they both looked at the tracks beneath them winding into the mountains beyond. The summer breeze blew through the pine trees and grass that covered the hills. Far off down the mountain, a train whistle blew, signaling it's laborious ascent into the Tehachapi Loop.

"Beautiful day isn't it honey."

"Yup, sure is Carl...look...that cloud looks like a bunny rabbit! See, straight up and to the left!"

"Wow, it does....it's perfect...even the cotton tail."

"Fuzzy little bunnies have to be a good omen huh?"

"I don't know Wendy, but it can't hurt."

"Yeah...I spose so..."

The train whistle blew again sounding like the mournful cry of some prehistoric creature as it echoed off the surrounding hills and valleys.

"You know what I see when I look down these railroad tracks Wendy?"

"No, what?"

"Infinite possibilities...that's what. I mean look at it, it just winds off into destinations unknown, adventures yet untold and stories that have yet to be written..."

"And you end up in Florida."

"No, I'm serious here...is there a mortgage waiting for us along these tracks? How about kids..."

"Fuzzy Bunnies?"

44

Carl smiled at Wendy. Her innocence and free spirit just jumped out and assaulted him for the umpteenth time since they met a year ago at Castaic lake. Carl felt his heart miss a beat as he fell in love with her all over again.

"Are we really happy here in Bakersfield Wendy?"

"I'm pretty happy."

"I mean really happy...you know like....look up at that hawk soaring on the air currents above that ridge...does your soul feel like that?"

"I guess so..."

"That would be a 'no'...I believe."

"Well Carl darling...I am happy but is that kind of happiness you're talking about even attainable? Sustainable? Realistic?"

"I don't know but it's something worth trying for....ya know?"

"Yeah but what do we do about it?"

"I don't know Wendy...maybe something will come our way."

"But will we recognize the opportunity when it comes?"

"I hope so...hey look at your fuzzy bunny cloud, it looks like a dragon now! It is even breathing fire!"

"From fuzzy bunny to dragon...there's a switch!"

"Maybe it's a sign Wendy."

"OK, I'm listening..." Wendy smirked a wry grin at Carl as she waited for his next statement.

"Well...we are pondering our lives and happiness and the road untraveled...maybe the bunny was symbolic of....ummm...our contentment with life even though we are not completely fulfilled and soaring like that hawk up there....and....uh.....the transformation into a dragon is telling us to burst forward through the fire and take control of our destiny and ummmm....not like.....uh...let anything stand in our way."

"You're an idiot."

"I'm serious here...." Carl cast his eyes down.

Wendy lifted his chin and her eyes met his.

"But you're a sexy idiot......and most importantly, you're my idiot." Wendy leaned over and kissed him passionately. The couple was soon making love under the brilliant blue sky with the breeze caressing their naked bodies.

The train was startling as it passed right beneath them. They could smell diesel and feel the ground vibrate as they lay tangled together in the grass on the hill above the tunnel.

"Wonder where this train is going?" Wendy looked deep into Carl's eyes.

"Dunno, destinations unknown..."

"Wendy continued looking at him. Carl pulled out from inside her and the pair got dressed without saying a word to each other but all the while their gazes were locked and each wore a mischievous grin.

"You ready Wendy?"

Wendy sang softly to Carl.

"Freedom's just another word for nothin' left to lose...nothin' don't mean nothin' honey if it ain't free..."

The two held hands. Standing on top of the tunnel they looked down at the train moving slowly below them.

"No looking back OK."

"No looking back."

Carl and Wendy jumped the few feet from the top of the tunnel onto the top of a boxcar. They lay down and looked up at the sky as the train rolled on to destinations unknown.

8:47 A.M.
JOHN SMITH'S FIRST DAY

"So whadja think of the big guy?"

"Amazing! He is the coolest!"

"Yeah he's all right huh. So ya ready to get started?"

John and Murphy were waiting in Sally Livingston's bedroom watching the red LED of her alarm clock change to 8:47 A.M.. Sally was supposed to start her new job today at 9:00 A.M. but John and Murphy made it so her alarm didn't go off at 6:00 A.M. like it was supposed to. They both watched with great delight as Sally opened her bleary eyes and upon seeing what time it was, flew out of bed in a hail of curses. John laughed as he heard her scream, "Life sucks! It just isn't fair!"

"I told you this was fun!" Murphy chuckled gently and his red cape flowed with each rise and fall of his shoulders.

Sally Livingston was an old girlfriend of John's who sucked him dry in every way. She was so good in bed that John chose to overlook the downward spiraling balance of his checkbook. He finally came home to an empty apartment only to find out from the landlord that he saw her and John's best friend leaving with a bunch of boxes around noon. Sally was responsible for John's ride on the number 17 bus for three years....

Sally always wanted to be in clothing design and today was supposed to be her first day working with one of the biggest fashion moguls in New York City.

"Hey Murphy, in a way....isn't what we did here sorta like karma getting her back for what she did to me?"

Murphy looked at John and smiled."Interesting observation there John......I knew you were perfect for this job."

A Little Conversation

"Hey Ted!"

"How ya doin' Bill?"

"Pretty good although it's gettin' rough around here . . . our gracious host really needs to quit smoking."

"I heard that! You should see all the drama down in the liver today! That was some bender he went on last night....geez....It's getting harder and harder to keep up with all the repairs."

Ted looked around at the cilia that lined the lung walls and saw all the black tar amid the healthy pink lining.

"Wow Bill, last time I was up here, there wasn't this much tar....my goodness..."

Bill sighed.

"Yeah Ted, I put in a request to the high and mighty brain cell contingent to work harder on getting our host to quit smoking but they're having a tough time...good 'ol subconscious is a tough nut to crack!"

"You can say that again Bill, we've been sending similar memo's upstairs only to receive the same frustrating brush off as well."

"Well Ted...I met my replacement....."

"Wow Bill, has it been seven years already?"

"Yup, time sure do fly...don't it now!"

"At least you have the benefit of living on in the new guy's memory."

"Yeah, I guess that's some consolation."

"Well we haven't survived this long without learning from our mistakes and working together...cellular memory goes back a couple billion years...too bad our human hosts can't figure this out huh."

"Amen brother Ted."

Bill sighed again.

"Hey fellas, what's the good word?"

"Hi Steve." Bill and Ted said in unison.

"Looks like we're having some problems here in the lungs Bill, everything OK?"

There was a smugness to Steve's tone that really irritated Bill.

"Oh, we have everything under control Steve, don't you worry."

Bill was indignant.

"Alrighty then...call me if you need me."

And with that, Steve took off.

Ted winked at Bill.

"Don't worry buddy, those stem cells are so up themselves...don't let him get to you."

"Yeah, they think they are so cool just because they can repair any cell in our host."

"Truth be told Bill...I wish I was a stem cell...wandering around fixing everything and not being a dedicated cell...." Ted trailed off.

"Not me Teddy boy, if I could have any gig it would be down there in the penis! Those cells are partying *all the time!"*

"Yeah Bill, but that crew down there is always wound up and so single minded....they never take a moment to just chill and relax, you can't even have a conversation with them...that's no way to live...is it?"

"Sure beats this job in the lungs, it's always damage control down here and everyone's always complaining!"

"Well it's no different down in the liver except everyone is drunk

50

most of the time...you try living with a bunch of pickled cells! Hell Bill, I come up here to see you and dry out a little bit!"

There was an awkward silence between the two cell buddies as they pondered their existence.

Finally, Bill broke the silence.

"You know Ted, it's amazing to me that after billions of years we finally create the perfect host and give these stupid humans all the tools they need to be healthy, happy and fulfilled and they keep wrecking all our hard work...it boggles the mind..."

"Yup, I remember all too well how hard it was for us when we were just single cells struggling so hard just to survive. When we started working together in harmony and began to band together into multicellular organisms, life got so much better. Remember when we created the first plant together?"

"Oh yeah Ted! The whole photosynthesis thing was so awesome! Remember how good that felt!"

"Boy do I! That sun felt so good...and the rejuvenating power it gave to the whole community....awesome...just awesome.."

"Yeah, it was onward and upward after that..fish, amphibians, reptiles, mammals...then we finally come up with the human design. I thought we'd finally arrived but nooooo....whoever let that doggone 'free will' into the mix had no idea how that would mess everything up huh?"

"Yup, ghost in the machine all right. Now we're left with all the mess...*and* cleanup! Well, chin up old pal, I heard that there is talks of a new, improved design on the drawing board so let's hope it will get better."

"It certainly can't get any worse Ted!"

"Well...I guess we shall see...anyway, gotta run. See ya later Bill, I'll stop by again before you are replaced and see you off OK. Thanks for the chat!"

"Cool Ted, have a good one. It was nice to get caught up with ya!"

THE HALCYON LIFE

Justin yawned and stretched his arms high above his head. He looked out across the parking lot of the *Mud Hut Motel* and watched the heat waves rise up with the dust as the 9:00 A.M. sun in Coober Pedy started its daily baking. Old Mr. Mac Gregor wandered by mumbling something about the heat frying what was left of his brain. Justin smiled and laughed to himself.

Justin was staying in the *Mud Hut Motel* until his house was built. He had been here for nearly three months and his house was nearing completion. He loved watching the tunneling machine dig out the rooms to his new dwelling. Everyone thought that Justin had lost his mind after he won the California lottery and announced that he was going to immigrate to Australia and live in Coober Pedy, the biggest Opal mining settlement in the country. From California to the middle of the South Australian outback...where the summer temperatures in Coober Pedy regularly hit 50 degrees Celsius and have been known to go as high as 60 degrees. All his friends were convinced that he was, well...nuts...and he would have to agree with them on some level as he was now going to live in an underground house in one of the harshest climates on the planet.

Justin smiled as he recalled the tourist information on the Coober Pedy website that boasted, *a diversity of people and activities guaranteed to keep the visitor engrossed for at least a day.* After reading that, he couldn't get on a plane fast enough. Yup, he was in heaven now......he could feel it with every breath of the harsh, hot air and with every swat at the relentless, never-ending swarm of flies that encroached on any orifice that promised even a hint of moisture.

Coober Pedy was officially named by the local Progress and Mining Association in 1922. The most widely accepted translation of the Aboriginal name is that 'coober' means either boy, uninitiated man or white man (all of which may well be interchangeable) and 'Pedy' means hole or rock hole. Thus, Coober Pedy is a description of what the local Aborigines regarded as peculiar activities (both mining and living underground) and so the town means 'white men down holes'.

After a small breakfast at the *Old Miners Dugout Café*, Justin headed across town toward his new house smiling broadly as he took in the sights and sounds of his newfound paradise. He always stopped by Crocodile Harry's place for a good yarn and a cup of terrible coffee (which Justin now couldn't wait to wake up for upon his retiring at night).

Crocodile Harry, this wonderful old lecher (his walls are festooned with the addresses of girls who he claims to have seduced) declares himself to be Arvid Von Blumentals, a Latvian Baron who was forced to leave his country after World War II. He claims to have worked as a crocodile hunter in Northern Australia before coming to Coober Pedy to fossick for opals in about 1975. Although his story seems implausible - a good piece of bush mythology - it is interesting to note that Roger Jose, the Hermit of Borroloola, who lived in a damaged 1000 gallon tank at Borroloola on the Gulf of Carpentaria in the Northern Territory until his death in 1963, reportedly sold his unusual accommodation to a crocodile hunter named Harry Blumental. Are these two one and the same person? Are all of Harry's larger than life stories true? Ahhh thought Justin...tune in next week when these and many other questions will be revealed. The irony was that even crazy old Crocodile Harry thought that Justin was nuts to leave California for this place but Justin was undaunted as he had never been happier. This was nirvana for him and he had no intention of ever going back...or *looking back* for that matter.

Justin's life before winning the lottery was a daily grind of traffic, a dead end job, too much coffee and Red Bull, shallow vapid friends and a fiancé who, once she got the engagement ring that cost Justin five paychecks (because her friend Marci's fiancé spent four paychecks and she would not be outdone) doled out the sex as if it were in a canteen and her and Justin were crossing the Sahara. Justin smiled as he recalled the look on her face when he announced that he would be leaving her to pursue a more 'civilized life' in an underground house mining for Opals in the outback. Justin swore he actually heard her shit her pants...there was a bit of an odor permeating the room as she realized her gravy train was leaving her high and dry to go back out into the dating jungle to snare another unsuspecting victim.

The short drive to his new house filled Justin with a sense of joy and purpose that he had never felt before. As he came to a stop in his driveway, his new Holden Commodore seemed to groan at the heat that was oxidizing the paint which was it's only defense from once again becoming one with the earth. As Justin stepped out of the car, the flies were just a swarmin' but he loved the sensation and looked at the hillside where his house was quite literally buried.

"Gidday there Yank!"

Riley Murray was taking smoko (Morning tea break) in the shade of the huge tunneling machine. Riley was all of four foot seven inches tall but handled the great tunneling beast as if he were ten foot tall and bulletproof.

"Gidday mate!" Justin still sounded goofy as he vocalized the Aussie slang.

"Join me for smoko mate?"

"Sure Riley, whatcha got today? Scones and cream?"

Justin fell in love with scones and cream and believed it to be a delicacy on the magnitude of the finest caviar one could purchase.

"Bloody well right mate, I know how much you like it so I had me wife make it up again this morning."

Justin sat down and indulged in the Nirvana that was scones and cream.

"So tell me yank, now that I'm almost done digging your house, I have to know...why are you here? I mean...bloody hell mate, this is a tough life out here. You could live anywhere with the money you won. The beach on the Gold Coast...hell...the beach...anywhere! I just don't get it."

Justin let the flavor of the scones and cream penetrate every taste bud on his tongue before he answered.

"Bars on my windows Riley."

Riley looked at Justin quizzically and lit a cigarette.

"OK mate, I give up...what does that mean?"

"Back in California, I lived in a good neighborhood but there was still crime and break-ins around the place so I put bars on all my windows. One day I woke up, opened the curtains and realized that I was in jail.....in my own house...that same day I got in my car to go to work and got stuck in a traffic jam which made me one and half hours late for work...and my job was only twelve miles from my house."

"It took you over an hour and a half to go twelve miles? That's bloody awful mate!"

"Yeah, and this was not just a one time deal...it happened frequently

Riley...then when I got to work it was the same old shit. Everything needed to be done yesterday and everyone was stressed out, standing around the water cooler complaining about how miserable their lives were and discussing the latest episode of 'Desperate Housewives'. It was at that moment I promised myself that if I ever had the chance, I was going to get as far away from all this as I possibly could and be happy with every sensation and cherish it with a vigor that was unparalleled...so...here I am. Opportunity finally knocked and I answered the call."

"Fair enough mate but why Coober Pedy?"

"When I was looking for my escape, I came across your tourism web page and it said that there was a diversity of people and activities guaranteed to keep the visitor engrossed for at least a day...well...I figure that once I have been engrossed for one day in all that Coober Pedy has to offer then I am truly free to live after that. Moment by moment...taking in every sensation, every emotion, every conversation, every scone with cream! "

"Well I ain't no philosopher yank but I guess I understand where you're coming from. I still think ya should've at least looked at the Gold Coast."

"Maybe someday Riley, but not today."

The two men talked, laughed and swatted at flies as the sun made its journey higher and higher into the afternoon sky.

Oprah Winfrey, Danielle Steel, Jenna Jameson,
A Beverly Hills gold digger, and two wives from Utah
and Kentucky decide the fate of men everywhere...
OR
The Case for Man...
OR
Women vs. Bob...

"Welcome, welcome . . . now if you will all just take a seat we
can get down to business."
The man who spoke stood at least eleven feet tall and was perfect in
every way from his sleek, v-shaped physique and perfect teeth to his
flawless skin and long blonde hair.
"You are no doubt wondering where you are and how you got here.
Let's just say that neither is of import at this present moment and
you will return to your lives as soon as we resolve the matter at
hand. You have all been brought here to discuss the current state of
affairs on earth and the most pressing matter of answering the
question regarding the necessity of continuing the male of the
species on your planet."
There were six women in the room and one man. The women
included, Oprah Winfrey (world renowned television personality),
Danielle Steel (world renowned romance novelist), Jenna Jameson
(world renowned porn star), Tiffany Minx (renowned Beverly Hills
gold digger), Audrey Wilkinson (renowned home maker in the small
town of La Verkin, Utah), and Stacy Jenkins (renowned town slut,

chronic pot smoker, boozer and...wife...from Winchester, Kentucky).
Rounding out the group was Bob Simmons (unrenowned,
unremarkable, unreliable and unbeknownst to him, the sole
representative of men all around the world).
The tall man was the only other being in the room with this group
and his name was,
Z^zK>7~~``~~ZxZxXUUUU``~~~^^^^^~~~ZzzzzzyX`~^ but let's
just call him "the tall man" for purposes of this documentation.
The tall man spoke.
"You are here because your species has finally reached a
technological crossroads. You have the capability now through
genetics and your knowledge of DNA to continue the human race
indefinitely and without disease or hardship into the next
millennium. Your sperm banks combined with stem cells and current
medical and scientific research has made the male of the species all
but obsolete. Believe me when I say this...we had high hopes for the
male and females of your species when we germinated the earth...but
the male has continued to be flawed to such an extraordinary extent
that we now feel we must step in. The women of your species have
shown the capability for nurturing and forgiveness and a genuine
desire to live in peace. That is why we are here. The women don't
need the men anymore now that the technology is at a level that can
sustain them without the physical contact that has, until this point in
time, been a necessity. All the other planets throughout the universe
that we have done this experiment on have prospered and learned
from their mistakes to quickly become valuable contributors to the
universe. You lot have continued to sell dignity to the highest bidder,
you are intolerant, racist, judgmental, warmongering, petty, selfish
and addicted to any form of instant gratification. Our researchers
have determined that the male of your species is the primary cause

59

of these problems by a factor of roughly 89%. You have had just over 2,000 years of enlightened thought to get this figured out and not only have you *not* learned anything, but quite frankly...it is getting exponentially worse! Now, we believe ourselves to be a fair and just race and, seeing as how we are basically your parents, we would like to hear both sides of the story from this group gathered here. Since men are 89% of the problem they are represented by Bob and Bob only. Since we see women as only 11% of the problem, they are represented by a six to one majority. Now your group represents the United States Of America. Each of our spaceships has a group with the exact same balance on it from each country on your planet so all cultures are represented. Any questions before we begin?"

The room was silent as the group sat, mouths agape, looking at each other as if maybe any second they might wake up from a bad dream. "OK then, why don't you get things started for us Bob. Why should men be allowed to continue on earth?"

BOB - B..b...but aren't you a man...a very tall man? Why do you want to wipe out your own kin?

THE TALL MAN - I am a highly evolved hermaphrodite capable of breeding and loving anyone of my kind so I have no ties to you other than the initial seeding of your planet. Please state your case and your case only.

Bob looked around the room and saw that all the women had fixated on him.

BOB - Ummmm...OK...well I'm not a bad man. I mean I go to work everyday and provide for my wife and daughter..isn't that worth something?

STACY - (snickering)Yeah, but I bet you think about her (pointing at Jenna) when you bang your wife.

60

Bob blushed and tried not to look at Jenna.

Jenna just stared straight at him and smiled wickedly.

OPRAH - Well, I've done shows where we discussed the fact that men are turned on visually and women emotionally so he is just acting typical if you ask me...nothing out of the ordinary there.

JENNA - Yeah but while he gets his jolly's, I get exploited.

TIFFANY - Exploited...please! If it wasn't for guys like Bob here, you wouldn't be partying at the Playboy mansion and driving a Ferrari...exploited my ass. I'll take your gig any day porn queen!

JENNA - Oh that's rich! I'm getting the moral high ground from a woman who exploits men's sexual needs for cars and jewelry

THE TALL MAN - Ladies, I believe Bob has the floor...if we could get back on topic..please continue Bob.

BOB - I have a question...does what I say here really affect all men on the planet earth?

THE TALL MAN - Yes.

BOB - (Swallowing hard) Well...that's an awful lot of pressure...I mean...I'm not, er...men aren't perfect...

STACY - Hhmmphh...you got that right...

AUDREY - I must say something here. I don't think all men are bad, my husband and I have raised five kids together, we have been married for 31 years and he still treats me with love and respect everyday. Not to mention that two of our kids are doctors, one works with the peace corps, one is a minister and the other owns a health food restaurant. They all are married, with kids and happy. If it wasn't for my husband providing the love and support both emotionally, spiritually and financially they would all quite possibly be very maladjusted and struggling in life.

DANIELLE - Well I think that finding the right man is the height of this existence, I mean true love like Audrey has is so rare but it must

61

be cherished and fought for!

OPRAH - I agree with that 100%. I mean, if men and women could just avoid all the pitfalls and stupid decisions in a relationship, communicate, have more realistic expectations and be more compassionate toward each others needs while still being independent...the world would be a much better place.

JENNA - Yeah but the sex always gets in the way. It's never enough, it's too much, I wanna do this, I don't wanna do that, lose weight, can we have a threesome cuz I'm bored...I mean, it never ends with men. They are never satisfied! Bob hasn't stopped trying to steal glances at my tits since we got here...

Jenna pulled her top down showing her breasts

JENNA - Get a good look Bob, here they are in all their glory!

Bob looked away and blushed.

AUDREY - Well this discussion is going nowhere....

TIFFANY - (Mumbling) What a slut.....

JENNA - I heard that bitch!

THE TALL MAN - Enough! Bob....

SCREE! SCREE! SCREE!

An alarm blared from the console where the tall man sat.

THE TALL MAN - Excuse me, there appears to be a problem on one of the other ships.

As the Tall Man left the room Bob looked at the women nervously.

BOB - Hey Oprah, what are three words that a husband dreads hearing from his wife when he comes home from work?

OPRAH - I don't know Bob, what?

BOB - On Oprah today....

Oprah rolled her eyes.

TIFFANY - That's funny there Bob o'! Well done!

AUDREY - I thought it was stupid....

Stacy leaned over to Jenna.

STACY - I love your work...maybe when this is all over...I've always had this fantasy about me and you...well...you know.

BOB - And I'm the degenerate on trial here!

STACY - Button it Bob and we might let you join us....oh wait...that's right, you ain't gonna be around much longer.

OPRAH - Will you all stop picking on Bob here! This is big time stuff here people! The extermination of men, can you really imagine a world without them?

DANIELLE - I sure can't.

TIFFANY - Yeah, there goes your career huh...come to think of it there goes mine and Jenna's as well...how ironic...

JENNA - Yeah how would you survive without your sugar daddy...slut.

Tiffany stands up.

TIFFANY - OK! That's it!

JENNA - (Standing up) Bring it on bitch!

STACY - You leave her alone you gold digging piece of shit!

OPRAH - Ladies please!

Jenna and Tiffany rush at each other and explode in a whirlwind of hair pulling and swearing.

The Tall Man re-enters the room and upon seeing the commotion points a small device at the fighting women and they are both teleported back to their chairs in a blinding flash of light.

THE TALL MAN - ENOUGH!

BOB - (Mumbling) And I'm the one on trial here...

THE TALL MAN - What happened! You are like children! I leave the room for three minutes and a fight breaks out....and between the women nonetheless! (Looking at Bob) Our research shows that you are the violent one in the species and yet we have this going on!

OPRAH - What was the alarm all about?

THE TALL MAN - We just lost a ship.

BOB - What happened?

THE TALL MAN - Apparently...our ship that was having the discussion group from the Middle East had an all out brawl break out and they took over the ship and....well...they blew it up. Anyway, we must finish here so we can come to a final decision. Continue Bob.

BOB - Well...

STACY- Wait! I have to ask a question here. A while back you said that you seeded our planet. Does that make you God?

AUDREY - He can't be God! He is clearly derivatively human! You speak blasphemy!

OPRAH - Now hang on a minute, nobody knows who or what God is for certain. We are all spiritual beings on the same journey.

TIFFANY - My herbalist says that you can see God in a cup of Chai Tea if you can learn to concentrate on the tea as your center.

DANIELLE - I've heard about that.......

THE TALL MAN - What are you talking about? I'm not God....and you certainly won't find him in a cup of tea! Look, I'm just trying to see if men deserve to continue given their past and present track record!

BOB - Now you see what us men have to deal with on a daily basis! I haven't got a word in edgewise since I got here! I've had to listen to a steady stream of illogical rants and crazy talk from women my whole life! Even my wife whom I love dearly drives me nuts....
Bob looked at the tall man and waved both arms in the air.

BOB - It's no wonder we go to war! It gets us out of the house!

OPRAH - Oh that's fresh, you know if you men just took a moment to try and relate to us with your feelings you'd understand us a lot better!

BOB - Right...I get it now, show our emotions and we will connect....*balony*! Cry in front of a woman and it is a one way ticket to pussyville! You lose their respect forever! Y'all have such a double standard that we can't possibly live up to! Be sensitive and we are a pushover. Be tough and we are a hard ass jerk! There is no middle ground! In fact Mr. Tall man, take me out now cuz you ain't never gonna fix this...EVER!

THE TALL MAN - Our purpose is to determine the truth of this matter.

TIFFANY - Well there's your truth stretch. Men and women will never get along. Although, on a side note...I'd like to see just what you are hiding in those trousers big boy.

JENNA - Oh my God, you did not just say that...

STACY - I guess gold digging knows no boundaries!

DANIELLE - I'm with Tiff.....curiosity you know...

AUDREY - Unbelievable.

OPRAH - Ladies, I do believe he is blushing...

BOB - Well there you have it, size does matter!

THE TALL MAN - Enough from all of you! I can't take it one moment longer! This is indeed hopeless at this present juncture. I will report that further research needs to be done before we can come to a final decision. In the meantime, enjoy what's left of your petty, squabbling lives!

And with that, the tall man pressed a button on the small device he held and the group vanished in a blinding flash.

Epilogue

The Tall man returns to his home on the planet, //<><><><>**^^^^^^^Beta=Gamma^^^^^^^**<><><><>\\ and walks through the door to find his partner waiting for him with dinner prepared.

THE TALL MAN'S PARTNER - How was your day?

THE TALL MAN - Terrible.....

THE TALL MAN'S PARTNER- You know...you forgot to take out the trash this morning.

THE TALL MAN - Oh will ya lay off me for once!

And with that, the Tall Man's partner throws the dinner from the cooking unit into the sink and storms out of the room crying. The Tall Man just lets out a long sigh.

A 24 HOUR SNAPSHOT OF
THIS THING WE CALL LIFE. . . A LIFE THAT
IS AS FLEETING AS A CLOUD OF SMOKE

Lazy-Boy Recliner, Nacho Cheese Doritos, Coors Beer, 54 inch plasma TV and *Three Stooges* reruns. This was the very definition of a perfect evening for Stuart Watson as he sat half drunk in a cloud of smoke from his third pack of the day.

The first two packs were finished off on the job today as he spread gravel on highway 14 in Southern California breathing in the hot tar fumes and waiting for the steamroller to push the rock into it's resting place, only to be dug out and broken by the eighteen wheelers daily travels.

Stuart was a chimney, smoking incessantly with only short pauses to drink some Gatorade or eat a sandwich. He even smoked in the Andy Gump, prompting the other workers to laugh as the smoke poured from the vents making it appear as if Stuart was taking a shit so big that it caused his rear to catch on fire.

Stuart had a good life by any standard. Twenty-nine years old, indestructible, and willing to take on the world. He got laid on a fairly regular basis and made enough money to have a nice apartment, beer, and smokes. It was no wonder that his physique was starting to show the inevitable signs of such blatant abuse. Dark circles started to creep out under his eyes like the moon moving in front of the sun during an eclipse and his once impressive six pack had switched places with the beer in the fridge.

Curly, Larry and Mo continued their antics as Stuart sat immersed in his own cloud of flickering smoke. When the commercials started, Stuart grabbed the remote and began channel surfing. Stumbling into a late night treat, Stuart put down the remote and began to smile as he watched Godzilla burn down Tokyo with his radioactive breath. Guys love Godzilla movies late at night almost as much as finding a James Bond flick.....both were mandatory late night drunken fare. Tonight there was the added bonus of the chick in the apartment below Stuart having loud sex with yet another random guy she met and at times was able to scream louder than Godzilla.

It was 1:11 A.M. on a Saturday night and no work tomorrow....monsters, guns and broads, 'it don't get no better than that' he thought. So Stuart leaned back, and despite the action on the TV and from the apartment below, he was soon fast asleep.

Stuart awoke to a local late night commercial where a man named Crazy Gideon who owned an appliance warehouse by the same name, was smashing TV's to demonstrate why he is crazy enough to give such low prices. Looking at the clock, the red digital glow burned 2:22 A.M. and the air in his living room smelled like his acrid cigarette and beer breath and the chick downstairs was still getting pounded....only now she had this high pitched whine that accompanied each orgasm. Lighting a smoke, Stuart stared through droopy eyelids at the television as Crazy Gideon was dragged, kicking and screaming from his store by a nurse in fishnets and high heels, all the while yelling and guaranteeing his low prices. Between the girl below him and the nurse in the hot outfit, Stuart was turned on. Grabbing the remote, he started to surf for a "Girls Gone Wild" infomercial to jack-off to. Two minutes after finding, and watching the girls going wild, Stuart was asleep in an orgasm-induced slumber.

Jasmine was the kind of girl that should never be allowed to drink Vodka.....it made her crazy lustful. Tom had left almost immediately after their three-hour marathon sex session and now she lay on her pillow staring at the ceiling, smoking a cigarette, feeling the wet spot under her grow cold. She smiled thinking about how she could hear Godzilla screaming from the apartment upstairs and she would answer with every thrust that Tom made inside her. Jasmine tried in vain to roll off the wetness but smiled as she realized that the whole bed was one big wet spot. Tom had done her right tonight.....she came 8 times. She stared at the digital clock that bathed the night stand in a soft, blue glow. The cunnilingus started at 12:33 and it was now 3:33 A.M.......almost three hours of relentless sex. She sucked at the cigarette, closed her eyes and smiled.

Cedric Teeter had been a janitor and maintenance man at the *bay view suites* for twenty-two years. He started every day with a cup of coffee and a smoke out on his balcony that featured a stunning view of the interstate, tumbleweeds and Joshua trees. If Cedric's life was a record, then this is where the scratch and inevitable skip is. With the final drag of his cigarette, just like a precision Rolex watch, Cedric would blow out the smoke, throw the cigarette on the ground, look up at the neon sign that blazed *bay view suites* and mumble, "bay view suites...in Barstow....my ass......." then he would glance at his watch and head back inside to cook two eggs (scrambled), some grits and have one more cup of coffee. This routine had never changed in twenty-two years. "It's good to have order and a routine..." Cedric would recite this mantra daily. It was certainly better than his old routine of drinking Jack Daniels all day and night and eating when he was hungry and

69

sleeping whenever he felt like it...no structure, no goals. Now he lived not only day by day, but minute to minute as he kept the alcohol demons at bay. Today was a new day for Cedric.... at least that's what he told himself every day for the last twenty two years. Cedric glanced at his watch and yawned, it was 4:44 A.M.. He forced a smile.....time to go to work.

Alex Campbell's eyes were burning and he woke up coughing and frightened. His room was full of smoke and the air was hot. He looked at his clock and saw that it was 5:55 A.M.. It was almost time to get up for school .....thirty five minutes before his Mom's alarm would go off and she would come in to gently wake him with a kiss on the forehead.

Alex had just turned nine. He was considered the class wimp at school and was picked on relentlessly by the other kids as he was much smaller in stature than everyone else in his grade. He couldn't play any sports as he was hopelessly uncoordinated. Dyslexia hampered his studies and to top it all off he wore coke bottle glasses that were always sliding down to the tip of his nose. By all accounts, Alex was well on his way to becoming a super nerd and all his peers made sure to remind him of this on a daily basis.

Living in the small town of Mojave, CA had its good and bad points for Alex. The F-117 and B-2 stealth bombers regularly flew over his house as they left Edwards Air Force Base for missions unknown. Alex loved flying so it was always a thrill for him to see the various planes around the Mojave skies. The big drag about small town life was the fact that everyone knew Alex as the town nerd and his father as the town loser. Alex had overheard hushed phrases like, "....that little boy will never amount to anything.....just like his Dad...." his entire life and would regularly cry himself to sleep as he recalled the incessant verbal.....and sometimes physical jabs of the day.

Alex coughed again and reached into his memory for what to do when there was smoke in the room......get down low....that was it! Alex rolled out of his bed and began crawling toward his bedroom door. The air was much better down low as he shuffled on his hands and knees. As he reached for the doorknob he stopped and recalled that it might be hot. Looking around, he spied a shirt laying on his floor. Alex grabbed the shirt, wrapped it around his hand, reached up, turned the knob and the door swung open. He crawled into the hallway beyond only to realize that the whole house was filled with smoke. Looking toward his parents room he saw that there were flames coming from underneath their door. Alex crawled down the hallway and turned through the entryway and toward the kitchen where he knew there was a fire extinguisher. The smoke was everywhere now and Alex quelled the fear that threatened to crush his spirit. Opening the pantry door, he grabbed the fire extinguisher off the wall....it was so heavy! With all his might he dragged it behind him as he crawled back toward his parents room.

When he reached their door he heard muffled wheezing and realized there wasn't much time.....he had to act now! Pointing the nozzle forward, he sprayed back the flames that were licking at the bottom of the door. He reached up and with the shirt wrapped once again around his hand, he turned the doorknob and the latch released allowing the door to swing open. Flames and smoke assaulted him as the door opened and he winced in pain as the heat burned his face and the smell of his singed hair wafted into his nostrils. Spraying the fire extinguisher in front of him, he managed to carve a path through the flames in front of him.

"Mom! Dad!"

Alex crawled through the room and continued to call out but received no reply. The smoke was so thick and Alex felt as if he would never make it out of there. Then through a break in the billowing smoke he spied his parents still laying in bed. Alex was now on his feet and running through the room possessed with the sole purpose of saving his parents. He smashed into the bed at full speed and bounced back onto the floor but was up in a heartbeat and was soon dragging his unconscious Mother from the room, down the hall and out the front door. Laying her on the sidewalk in front of the house, he raced back into the inferno. Now Alex could hear wood cracking and a loud crash from the attic which could only mean that the roof was starting to collapse. With superhuman speed and determination he entered the bedroom that was becoming his father's tomb. He slid on the floor now just like a batter into home plate and skidded to a stop at the foot of the bed. Reaching up he grabbed his Dad's arm and threw him over his shoulder and stood up in one fluid motion. Alex ran down the hall as the roof shuddered and fell in behind him as he dashed toward the door like Indiana Jones escaping the Temple of Doom.

As Alex dashed through the front door and out into the driveway he saw the gaping mouths of his mother and ten firefighters staring at the small boy with a man three times his weight slung over his shoulder like a sack of potatoes. Suddenly Alex felt his Dad's full weight as the adrenaline wore off and he collapsed on the driveway as the firefighters rushed forward to help him and his father.

Just before Alex drifted into unconsciousness, he heard one firefighter say, "Wow, I ain't never seen a kid so strong and brave! He is truly a giant among men!"

Alex managed a smile and peacefully drifted off into the cool of the morning sunrise.

Tucker Franklin or "Tuck" as the fellas called him, kicked open the door to the small shack and rushed in with his comrades shouting, "GET DOWN! GET DOWN NOW!" With machine guns sweeping the single room he saw the fear in the eyes of the old man in the corner behind an overturned table. Despite the fear he saw in those eyes, he was sure that he could still see the hatred that was still smoldering on the surface of the old man's stare.

"All Clear! Move out!"

Tucker's commander gave the order and the squad peeled out back through the front door of the hut and back into the Iraqi sun which, with all their gear felt more like a kiln from which there was no escape. Tucker's squad walked down the street and rendezvoused with the other half of their unit.

"Eighteen hundred-hours sarge, and the village is clear."

"Good work son, let's move out." And with that, Sergeant Harker jumped into the hummer. Pointing straight ahead, the driver pulled forward in a cloud of dust and Tucker wished he was riding and not staying behind to patrol this rat shit, hell hole until his relief came.

BOOM!

Tucker and his squad hit the ground as the concussion from the roadside bomb blew the hum-v and it's passengers into oblivion. All that was left was a crater and the shell of the vehicle. The passengers.......his friends and brothers in arms....were gone. A single tear rolled down Tuckers face as the smoke from the smoldering funeral pyre blew past his face.

Colin Clark squinted as he stared ahead down the road. The smoke from the sugar cane fire was so thick that he was driving with his headlights on low beam and having a really difficult time

73

negotiating the highway. It was 2:22 A.M. and Colin had just finished his shift at the Glenmore Pub as the head bartender. Between the smoke he breathed all night in the bar and the sugar cane fire, his lungs felt as if they were going to explode. His yellow Mitsubishi van continued to trundle down the road that was affectionately known by the locals as the "Rocky Road." This was the road that connected the town of Rockhampton to Yeppoon in Central Queensland, Australia. The road lived up to its name too. A pitted patchwork of uneven pavement and potholes made the drive hard on the kidneys and there was no such thing as driving with your morning cup of coffee.....many had tried and all arrived at work with the dreaded crotch burn and stain broadcasting their coffee debacle.

Colin's eyes were tired from the constant straining, stress and burning from the smoke. For just one split second he closed his eyes and squeezed out gritty tears which felt so good on his dry scorched eyes...

BANG!

The van shuddered. Colin planted his foot on the brakes and skidded to a stop on the side of the road. He jumped out of the car and looked through the smoke to see a kangaroo lying at the side of the road. "Oh shit....."

Walking toward the stricken roo, Colin could hear it wheezing and saw its sides heaving as the blood from a mortal head wound drained into the dirt. Just as he reached the creature he heard one final gasp and it was over.

"Dammit! Just what I need.......what the?"

Colin saw the joey crawl from its deceased mother's pouch and look him right in the eye as if to accuse him of his new status as an orphan. Colin gently picked up the baby roo and walked back to the van.

74

"I got ya little one, you're gonna be all right mate."
Wrapping the joey in his jacket and laying him on the passenger's
seat, he started the van and pulled back onto the highway.
"Well little buddy, looks like you have a new home."

    Jerry crossed Leicester square in the pouring rain and opened the
door to the *Cork & Bottle* restaurant and champagne bar. Descending
the narrow spiral staircase, he was greeted by Nadine who was a
stunning French woman that should be on the cover of every skin
mag from London to California but was instead working underneath
Leicester square in central London.
"Hallo Messier, may I show you to your table."
They walked to the back of the establishment to Jerry's "spot" which
was an alcove that for all intent and purpose was like a little cave
with a very low, rounded ceiling and a dank musty smell.
"The usual Mr. Jerry?"
"Yes, thanks Nadine."
Jerry came here every day at exactly 5:05 P.M. after work to
celebrate another half-assed attempt at feigning that his life was
good. Lighting a cigarette, he watched Nadine bring his glass of
champagne to him and was immediately fantasizing about hearing
her coo in his ear that she wanted him inside her right now.
"Ten pounds fifty messier Jerry."
Jerry produced his wallet from his wet jacket.
"Here you go Nadine."
He watched the sway of her hips as she left his "cave" and faded
back into the thrall at the bar.

Judy Perkins hated the cold, but this particular morning was testament to the beauty that only God could lay out before her. She was galloping through the snowy foothills of the Sandia mountains on her horse Arrow, with the brisk morning air stinging her lungs as she raced between the snow-covered pine trees. As the great beast snorted in rhythm with its strides it looked like smoke was blasting from its nostrils like some sort of steam driven super horse. Judy pulled on the reigns bringing the mighty animal to a stop and waited patiently for her dog to catch up. Soon the familiar sound of Chico, a beautiful collie drew nearer and finally the dog rounded the bend in the trail panting plumes of smoke as its warm breath met the cold winter air. Judy looked out over the foothills and up to the snow-covered mountain top. Pulling her glove back she glanced at her watch, 11:11 A.M., still plenty of time to enjoy this glorious morning before she had to return home. Judy spurred Arrow and the trio once again took off through the snow-covered New Mexico hills.

The headlights of the range rover lit up the small village in the Pursat province of Cambodia. It was 2:22 A.M. in the morning and two men were hunched over in front of their range rover bathed in the headlight beams.

" Whatever you do.......don't cut the green wire......."
A small river of sweat was now flowing down Peter Dempsy's forehead as he slowly negotiated the wire cutters through the spaghetti of multi colored circuit leads.
"I know! I know! Get off my back! You think this is easy ham hands! Geez......."

Peter and Bobby, "ham hands" Reynolds had been best friends for five years now. They met in London when they were both training in the same bomb disposal unit and had been together ever since. Bobby was a genius when it came to bomb tech and Peter was the finesse on the team. Together they had never met a bomb or mine that they couldn't diffuse safely. After working in the middle east for the last four years they decided to put their talent to use in areas of the world that needed help with clearing minefields. Innocent people were regularly losing limbs or dying as a result of minefields. One minute their children are playing, the next they have no legs.

Peter and Bobby had run into a doozy today. An unexploded bomb that had become dislodged when the side of the hill where it was buried collapsed, sending the bomb rolling into a small village. The kids looked on in awe as the two cursed at each other while they worked on disarming the lethal beast.

"Let's go to Cambodia you said....help people out you said..."

"Shut up Bobby....you're sure I cut the red wire right?"

"Yup."

"OK....here goes nothing...."

Peter cut the red wire and it made a popping noise followed by a shower of sparks.

"Oh shiiittt!" Bobby yelled as he jumped back.

Peter just stared at the smoking bomb and smiled.

"Looks like you were right....it was the red wire ham hands."

Chris and Gary had partied massively the night before with the guys from the U2 squadron. The rice alcohol, Soju had made for a huge night of drinking, dancing and strip bars in the town of Osan, South Korea. Being musicians in a rock band over there to entertain the troops on the base, Chris and Gary got the royal treatment from the soldiers, especially after their twenty minute medley of "Sweet Home Alabama" and "Freebird" earlier at the show. Now the pair were making their way across Osan Air Force Base in the driving winter wind as flurries of snow blew around them like so many gnats.

"You're never going to light that dude."

Gary was referring to Chris' futile attempts at lighting a smoke in the howling wind.

"Oh, I'll get it......I have to....it's a *must do* hangover helper Gary." And no sooner had Chris said that when there was a slight break in the gale and the cigarette sparked to life.

"Told ya."

"Man, last night was a blast, those guys were awesome!"

"Yeah and I can't believe we get a tour of the U2 unit today!"

It was 7:07 A.M. and Chris and Gary were on their way to a rendezvous at hanger 17 to meet the guys in the U2 squadron and see what was involved in keeping one of the world's most tried and true spy planes airborne.

Upon arriving at the hanger, they were greeted by Steve and Jerry who, despite the Soju-fest, looked bright and chipper. This was in stark contrast to Chris and Gary's messy hair under baseball caps, dark circles under the eyes, death warmed up look.

"Mornin' boys!" Steve said with a big shit-eating grin.

"Ready to see some serious shit?"

"Ready for Freddy dude!" Chris was thrilled at the prospect of seeing the U2 up close as he had always been into airplanes growing up with a father who was a pilot.

"Then let's get going!" Jerry turned and opened the door to the hangar and the quartet walked through.

For the next 3 hours, Chris and Gary got the grand tour. They let them eat the "food in a tube" that the pilots had to eat as each mission could last ten to fifteen hours. They also let them sit in the cockpit of the plane which is incredibly snug, especially since the pilots wear a space suit due to the extreme altitude that the plane flies at. After trying on the space suits which Gary got briefly trapped in due to a snagged zipper, they went to the control tower to watch a U2 landing. Because of the U2's design, the plane has to land nose first and once it is on the runway, the pilot gently lowers the tail of the plane and cruises to a stop. Because the landing is so difficult, there is a super charged chase car equipped with a radio that follows the plane and talks the pilot down to the tarmac. The chase car is usually a mustang, trans-am or similar juiced up American muscle car. The whole landing was thrilling to watch for the two musicians in the tower.

After the thank you's and goodbyes, a plan was set into place to party again that night. Chris and Gary headed into the town off base to get some local Kimchi, all the while talking about how great it is to be a musician and experience such wonderful fellowship no matter where they went in the world.

Jamie Corkins couldn't believe this vacation so far. She was somewhere in the bush about 100 miles north east of Cape Town in South Africa. It was 11:11PM. The rain was pouring down relentlessly, and she had both her arms up a cow's vagina trying to turn the calf around and deliver it safely. Only six hours ago she was sipping a pina colada in a quaint bar in Cape Town after a grueling 16 hour flight from Melbourne, Australia. Halfway through the refreshing drink, her friend Melinda who worked with the red cross came rushing up with a local man who was very distraught.

"Jamie! We have to leave right away, this man's cow is having trouble.....she's about to deliver and there's a problem.....hurry!"

Jamie was a veterinarian back in Melbourne here to relax and visit Melinda who was one of her best friends from school. Melinda spoke the native languages and had helped quite a lot of unfortunate villagers in her travels around Africa. Today was no exception. If this man and his family lose this cow and the calf it would be devastating so before she knew what was happening, Jamie was in Melinda's land rover heading into the bush.

Now as she pushed and pulled on the calf the mother cow was starting to freak out a little bit and kick with her back legs.

"Melinda! You have to keep her still! Get more help or something, I'm almost there!"

And just then, Jamie got the baby calf got into position, the mother cow pushed and out came the head. Jamie helped pull it out of the cow and within 20 seconds, it was all over. Covered in afterbirth and mud, Jamie held the newborn calf and the man was praising her in his native tongue with tears in his eyes. Melinda said, "he is very grateful for you, he says you are his angel."

The man handed Jamie his lit cigarette and although Jamie had never smoked she accepted it and took a long drag as the baby cow lay curled in her arms.

Jeff Benson was flying the Beechcraft Bonanza at nine thousand feet above the New Mexico desert. Passing over shiprock he banked slowly to the left and began to drop in altitude in order to come back around and take some pictures of the great rock. It was 3:33 P.M. by the digital clock in the dash of the cockpit and he could see the sun starting to make its final journey toward the horizon causing shiprock and the surrounding desert to start to turn orange and purple as only the southwest can do. As the plane came around, Jeff noticed puffs of smoke coming from below and saw a group of Indians around a fire. One man was covering and uncovering the fire with a blanket causing the smoke to rise in various intervals and duration. Some were big smoke clouds and others were smaller and closer together. Jeff realized that it was Navajo smoke signals but from his service in the Navy, he noticed that they were actually sending morse code on this day. Jeff flew around again and waved from the plane as he flew over the group. He wanted to let them know he got the message which had said, "Blessed are you to fly like the bird on this beautiful day." Jeff couldn't have agreed more.

Tsang drew in a deep breath and the sweet aroma of the incense caressed his nostrils. He was leaving...he just can't seem to find peace...even among the Buddhist monks deep in the mountains of Nepal. He had announced that he would leave at dawn. It was now five minutes after five in the morning and the faint light of the rising sun was starting to push back the darkness. He stood in front of the hazy smoke from the burning incense and accepted his fate, he would never be happy or content. The Buddhist master had told him that peace must come from within and that it is within the stillness that lies the secret to happiness but Tsang paid a lot of money to come here and he wanted quicker results, not something as intangible as this. What a waste of time he thought. The steady thrum of his private helicopter was coming closer and soon he would be back to his position as vice president of marketing at Sony back in Tokyo. He would find happiness he thought...especially since he had his assistant book a three-hour session with Jade at the bath house....oh yes, he would find happiness...if only for a couple hours at a time.

    Gerald Adams lit his cigarette, took a long drag and pulled the handle of the *double diamond* progressive slot machine. As the reels spun in front of him, he glanced at his watch, 4:44 P.M. He had been gambling for fourteen hours straight. He was on his way back from Denver on a run from Los Angeles when he stopped at *Whiskey Pete's* on the Nevada, California border to see if he could win some big money.

    Gerald's son, Tyler had been diagnosed with cancer two months ago and since their insurance company, Kaiser Permanente refused to pay for treatment citing a clause in the policy that pointed to a pre-existing condition, Gerald and his wife Lynn had been left with a sick child and mounting medical bills for mediocre and indifferent care at the county hospital.

    Gerald drove a big rig and had taken any and all jobs he could get so the last two months were spent on the highways of America while his wife and son were at home, his wife fighting the insurance company on her own as they couldn't afford a lawyer and Tyler fighting for his life. Once a day, Gerald would call home to talk to them but once a day was all his broken heart could take as he heard Tyler's voice grow weaker and weaker and Lynn's voice grow more and more weary. So here he sat in front of a slot machine hoping to make a big score and by some miracle be able to get Tyler the treatment he so dearly needed.

    Gerald looked at the credits on the slot machine. He had 5 left......just enough for one more spin and then his whole paycheck would be gone. He took a drag of his smoke and said a silent prayer

82

and pulled the handle. He blew smoke out of his nose and it became a cloud in front of the spinning reels. The first reel stopped on the jackpot symbol and Gerald's heart jumped inside his chest. The second symbol was also a jackpot and time slowed down for Gerald as he only needed one more and he would win 4 million dollars and Tyler would be able to get the treatment he needed.........

"Shit! Shit! Shit! I don't fuckin' believe this bullshit!"
Aurora just scowled at the blackened pot roast in front of her, arms frenetically fanning the smoke that continued to pour from the oven and the pan that held the doomed roast. She was quite a sight batting at the smoke with big mitten style potholders on the end of her skinny arms. All the while dressed in a catholic schoolgirl outfit complete with pigtails and six inch shiny black pumps.
"Well this is perfect.......just fuckin' perfect........"
Three hours ago, Aurora had been curled up in her pajamas with a box of See's chocolates and the season premier of Southpark when her husband came home earlier than she expected and freaked out.
"What the hell are you doing? Is this what you do all day? Sit around and watch cartoons!? It's 8P.M. for God's sake!"
"Southpark is more of an adult cartoon.....maybe you should check it out with me....it's really funny."
"Adult cartoon huh? Well that doesn't apply to you since you are only twenty-five going on fourteen! Now get off that couch and fix me something to eat, I've had a bad day and you need to earn your keep around here!" And with that, Richard Weinstein, sixty-two, and one of the richest men in all of Manhattan stormed out of the room and left his trophy wife in stunned silence.
"Well, I can fix this......" Aurora got up off the couch and sauntered

to the bedroom shedding her clothes as she walked.

When Richard saw her leaning back on the doorframe to the bedroom, one arm raised, back arched, naked and purring he said, "No this ain't gonna fly babe, I'm hungry and you need to fix me something.....now."

"But baby, you know I don't know how to cook....we always eat out....."

It was true, there was no chapter in the gold digger's handbook that covered cooking.

"Well you better learn....quick."

"But I don't wanna Ritchie..." She purred.

"Nope, not gonna fly tonight. Food. Now. And put something sexy on while you do it. . . I like the schoolgirl outfit."

Aurora was stunned. She walked back to the living room, replacing the fallen clothes to her body.

This was quite the conundrum for her. If something didn't involve cheerleading, sex or shopping she was lost. Time for the tantrum. Aurora stormed back to the bedroom.

"I'm not going to cook for you because.....um...because I don't have to and what's more.....I could break a nail and you don't want that on your conscience!"

Aurora was quite proud of that big statement and remembering how to say conscience.

Richard just smiled at her

"Two words Aurora......PRE - NUP."

Mitch, Jason and Andrew were going eighty miles per hour on the interstate, laughing and whooping it up as they raced toward the Metallica concert in Phoenix.

"Man this is so gonna rock tonight dude!" Jason was smiling as he blew smoke through his nose and sucked it back into his mouth all while driving his beat up GTO down the road.

"Yeah man, and with weed this good you just know it's gonna fuckin' go off man!" Mitch was sprawled across the back seat with a joint hanging from the side of his mouth and air drumming to the song, "Master of puppets" that was blaring through the stereo.

"Like, what time is it dude?" Andrew was so stoned that he had struggled with the seatbelt for the last five miles trying to figure out how it had caught and pinned his arm to the door handle. When he finally got free, both Mitch and Jason showed their solidarity with a collective, "Dude.... that was awesome!"

"Dude, it's like exactly seven minutes past seven....wow that's like totally cosmic ya know....like seven is a lucky number and the time is like two sevens so we are gonna have twice the luck man..." Jason was proud of his observation.

"That means Metallica is gonna rock twice as hard!" Mitch made the universal sign of "metal" with his hand and pumped it to the beat of "Enter Sandman" that now blared through the speakers.

All three friends collectively yelled, "Fuck yeah!" and drove on down the highway to the show of a lifetime.

Sally Jones put the last log in the fireplace and lit the gas, smiling as the flames jumped from the gas pipe and licked at the wood. Tonight the temperature was supposed to drop to twenty-one degrees in Saint Louis. It was nine minutes past nine according to the blue glow of the digital clock on the VCR and Sally sat back in the recliner, ready to watch the DVD of "Pretty Woman" that Joyce lent her from the office. Just as she took her first sip of wine she choked on the smoke that had filled the room. She jumped from the recliner and saw that the smoke was billowing from the fireplace. She had forgotten to open the flue and the smoke had no place to go but back into the house. Grabbing the fire poker, she coughed as she pushed against the handle to the flue and it slammed open with a bang sending the smoke back up the chimney.

Kevin Jenkins wiped the sweat from his brow...he was bombing big time. He stared out into the dark lounge and heard a person cough from somewhere out there in the smoky haze. The Kevin & Kozmo show was dying a slow, painful death tonight...in fact this whole small tour of comedy clubs that Kevin had been on for the last three weeks was dying a slow death, just like his beat up old Dodge van that he drove to barely make it from gig to gig. Kevin was a ventriloquist and Kozmo was his puppet who was a stoned out hippie complete with Tye Dye shirt, round glasses and a joint hanging from the corner of his mouth. His act killed in high school but now he was in the hard reality of drunken audiences full of chain smoking hecklers.

"So Kozmo, what does a Hindu do when he finishes his joint?"

"Like nothin' man....he just waits for it to be reincarnated.....like he never runs out of weed man!" Kozmo was shaking his head and looking around the audience for a reaction while Kevin felt a river of sweat run down his back under his shirt. Kevin caught sight of the clock in the wings of the stage, it was 10:10PM and he still had twenty minutes left to go.

"Hey Kevin."

"Yeah Kozmo."

"Like, how does a Buddhist change a lightbulb?"

"I don't know Kozmo, how."

"Just like everyone else but the lightbulb has to want to change."

Again Kozmo scanned the audience for a reaction.

"You suck dude!"

"Yeah, get off the stage.....and take your stupid puppet!"

Kevin was at a loss so he decided to light a cigarette to calm his nerves.

"Hey man....you gonna light my smoke too?" Kozmo was looking at Kevin.

"Sure Kozmo, but don't you think you've smoked enough for a lifetime?"

"What's one more hit man?"

This was not part of Kevin's act but he was desperate.

"Here you go buddy."

Kevin lit the fake joint that dangled from Kozmo's wooden mouth and heard a few chuckles from the audience.

"Like wow man....thanks for hookin' a brother up. Now having your hand up my ass doesn't seem so weird."

More chuckles from the darkness.

Kevin looked out into the audience and in a split second, the paint on Kozmo went ablaze in a blinding flash and left Kozmo with a burnt face and no hair. Kevin also had no more hair on his arm and before he could even begin to react, the fire was out.

Thinking fast, Kevin looked at Kozmo who looked back at him and said, "Wow man....like that was some potent weed!"

The audience went berserk with laughter and all Kevin could think about was how to get enough money to burn a different puppet every night for his new show.

Harry Freeman lay in the hotel bed smoking the cigarette that Lynette Peterson gave him. Harry didn't smoke but he was having a good time tonight, especially after that great ventriloquist show and flaming stoner puppet in the lounge of the Holiday Inn where he and Lynette were staying for the convention.....oh.....and the sex with Lynette wasn't too bad either. In fact it was the best he ever had. He had been fantasizing about this hook up for a long time. Harry was 46 years old, married with four kids and sold tile for a living. Lynette was 27 years old and was the receptionist for the tile showroom....and every man's fantasy who worked there. Harry had sex with his wife once every two or three months if she was feeling generous and up until ten minutes ago, he had been faithful. Between the drinks, show and Lynette's "Daddy complex," it just all seemed to work out for him tonight coming to an amazing climax at 11:11 P.M. in room 452 at the Holiday Inn off the US highway 75 in Denison Texas. Harry lay back deep in the pillow as he watched Lynette come out of the bathroom, hips swaying in stockings and high heels with a look of pure sex on her face.
"Ready to go again big boy?"
Harry took a drag from the smoke and slowly exhaled.
"Yup." Was all he could muster up.

The fire department arrived on the scene at 10:10 P.M. and the building had become an inferno. The Los Angeles office of Kaiser Permanente health insurance was awash in flames and smoke with the skeleton of a big rig truck jutting out of the front of the building like an arrow in a warriors chest. The fire chief, Brent Castro watched as his crew beat back the flames and he could see that they had recovered the charred body from the truck. An EMT that he knew named Tim Marshall was wheeling it over to the waiting ambulance.

"Did you find some ID for the driver Tim ?"

"Yeah, guys name is Gerald Adams, next of kin is his wife Lynn. He has one child named Tyler, I've sent a black and white to inform them of what has happened although the press might beat us to them.....look at all these fuckin' helicopters....nothing brings 'em out like a good fire huh."

Brent just looked at the charred body of Gerald Adams and wondered what could push a man to do what he did tonight.

"What a shame Tim....what a shame....."

"Just another day Brent....just another day."

Jane sat on her bed with the pillow hugged tightly to her chest, the clock at her bedside glowed 11:11 P.M.. She had been weeping for three hours and the pillow was wet from her tears. The ashtray next to her bed was full of cigarettes and smoke from one that she hadn't quite extinguished sent a lone trail of smoke curling slowly into the air. It was over. Her marriage of 11 years was over. She got the call from her husband three hours ago and although it wasn't a surprise as they had been having problems for years, it was the finality of it all and the knowing that it was done that hit home for Jane. She had always wanted the fairy tale and for eight of the ten years they were married it was...until her one drink every night after work turned into two, then three until finally becoming a monster that she had no control over.

Her husband was a good man but even he had his limits. Last month's D.U.I had sealed the deal for him. He had tried repeatedly to help her to no avail and her constant stonewalling and anger pushed him so far away that there was now nothing left for him to do but move on. Jane reached for the bottle of Vodka on the night stand, took a swig and lit another smoke. Walking to the window, she looked out over the ocean from their condo in Redondo Beach, California. He didn't understand, that's all....she was in control....Jane took another big drink from the bottle.....she didn't need him anyway.

Erik plodded through the snow as he walked home after a huge night of partying at Cantina West in Helsinki, Finland. It was 10:10 A.M. and he smoked his last cigarette as he trudged on wondering if that girl really was his soul mate. They had only met last night and were both pretty lit up on tequila and vodka but there was an instant attraction and they spent the night dancing, laughing and talking. Toward the end of the night, she announced that he was her soul mate and Erik was completely taken aback but relieved and overwhelmingly happy all at once. She then kissed him very gently and excused herself to go to the bathroom. Erik sat alone in the corner table they had occupied all night. He waited and waited for her to return but she never did. Soon the club's disco lights shut down, the house lights came up and the bouncers were walking him to the door and outside into the snow. Where did she go, he wondered? Why was his heart breaking after only knowing this strange woman for six hours. He would see her again....he was sure of it.....at least he hoped he would see her again......he took a final drag on the cigarette, tossed it into the snow and sighed.

Ivan sat on the cold chair waiting. It had been 45 minutes and he was bored and frustrated. He was totally jonesing for a cigarette as he had been at the hospital for three hours now, what with the waiting room, x-rays and everything. Now it was 12:12 P.M. and he had to rejoin the others in front of the Kremlin...all he had was a fucking cough anyway, what could the damn doctor be doing? Just when Ivan thought he was gonna lose it, the door opened and doctor Vlad came in.

"Well Ivan, I'm afraid I have some bad news.....you have lung cancer....I'm really sorry."

Ivan just stared at the doctor in disbelief.

Stuart Watson sat back in his Lazy-Boy recliner with a fresh bag of nacho cheese Doritos, and turned on the big 54-inch plasma television, it was 1:11 A.M.

Opening a Coors and lighting a cigarette, he found the *Three Stooges* and laid back in the recliner for another evening.

Naughty Nympho Nurses

Jimmy was a doctor of proctology.

Crystal was Jimmy's nurse by day and a stripper by night.

You can see where this is going.

The end.

Suicide Isn't An Option.......Today

Bill Taggart felt the cool breeze blow through his hair, chilling his sweat soaked forehead. The cold November air made him feel so alive.....if only for the briefest of moments. Looking down at the alley far below, a taxi picked up another drunk from Doc Holiday's bar and then sped off down second street to destination unknown. The lights of the Cal Neva casino pulsed rhythmically off the building across from where he stood.. . high atop the roof of the casino's parking garage.

Six months ago, Bill was so happy. A great family, fantastic job and a 1975 Corvette parked in his garage which made an appearance every Sunday when he would take his wife to Lake Tahoe. They would cruise around the lake with the T-top off and after a great lunch at one of their favorite haunts, they would park overlooking the lake and make love as the sun glistened off the water. Bill's life was right where he wanted it.....and more.

The Pittsburgh Steelers won by 24 points, crushing the Miami Dolphins. As the final whistle blew, Bill felt the hand of Luigi Leoni grab his shoulder.

"Well pal, looks like we have a problem now."

"I can get the money....I..I..I..swear....I just need to um...go to an ATM and get it."

"Yeah yeah pal. Look, I'm gonna go take a piss and when I come back youse is gonna pay me something in good faith or Vinnie and I are gonna have to take matters into our own hands and youse is gonna be really late for dinner....like a lifetime late....pal."

Luigi slapped Bill's cheek and smiled. Turning away, he leisurely

93

strolled across the casino towards the bathroom with Vinnie in tow. Bill's mind was racing as he walked from the sports book inside Harrah's and out the side door to go across the street to the ATM at the liquor store. There was no money in the account....passing the liquor store, he walked up the stairs of the parking garage at the Cal Neva hotel crying softly as he thought how different his life would be right now if the Dolphins had won. After all, they were a lock according to his "reliable" source. He bet the last of his family's savings and the corvette in an act of desperation to pull out of the debt that he owed to the biggest crime family in Reno. Gambling had taken a hold of Bill four months ago and he had brought shame and ruin to himself and his family quickly and decisively.

The cool breeze had stopped, the air was crisp, and the alley far below was silent and still. Bill readied himself for the jump and whispered, "I love you" to his wife and four-year-old son as he stepped silently off the edge.

As Bill fell silently toward earth, Johnny Jackson hurriedly turned his truck into the alley behind the Cal Neva for his ritual smoke out. Johnny always got stoned halfway through his shift and on Mondays his delivery route took him to this side of town. As it happened, tonight Johnny was transporting mattresses to the Sit & Sleep store. As he came to a stop and rustled through his glove box for his stash, he felt a shudder and heard a thud in the back of the truck. Johnny jumped out of the cab and climbed up the side of the truck bed to see a man laying comfortably on top of all the mattresses laughing hysterically with tears in his eyes.

"Well fuck me! I can't even kill myself right!"

"Hey dude....are you OK? Where did you come from?"

" I fell out of a UFO....."

"Wow man.....that is trippin' for sure! I thought I saw a bright light

94

outa the corner of my eye dude! I see strange stuff all the time when I'm on the chronic!"

Bill laughed even harder at the young man whose penchant for being constantly stoned was his savior on this night. As the stoner stared at him, Bill realized that the problems he had faced mere seconds before were still looming above him. The Leoni brothers were still going to want their money and at the very least, going to give him a permanent limp.

As Bill climbed out of the truck, Johnny kept mumbling, "whoa dude, this is like....so freakin' me out man."

"Thanks for the catch dude."

Johnny climbed back into the truck, started the engine and said, "No problemo dude, hope them aliens didn't probe you....well....you know....later bro."

And with that, Johnny the stoner savior drove out of the alley and merged into traffic, leaving Bill in a cloud of diesel smoke. Bill raised his head to the sky, inhaled deeply and closed his eyes. As he stood there, he became very calm and realized what he almost lost tonight and vowed that he would take responsibility for his actions and make things right no matter what the price....he owned this situation. He told himself this and a great calm washed over him. As he slowly opened his eyes and took another deep breath, he saw a piece of paper gently floating down from the sky. He watched it slowly come to rest at his feet and saw that it was a lottery ticket. Bill bent down to pick it up and walked out of the alley and into the liquor store next to Doc Holiday's bar. He handed the ticket to the clerk and took a deep breath as he watched him scan the bar code. The clerk's eyes lit up and he said, "You have won sir!"

"How much?" Bill was incredulous.

"Ninety-seven thousand!"

Bill just stood there, mouth agape as it sank in. He owed the Leoni's ninety-six thousand. As if on cue, Luigi walked out of Harrah's and spotted him in the liquor store.

"Hey! You gettin' my money or what!?"

Bill walked out of the store as the clerk looked on with great interest.

"Got it right here Luigi, including a little thousand-dollar tip for being so understanding!"

Bill handed him the ticket as Vinnie strolled up adjusting his crotch.

"What the fuck is this Billy boy?"

"It's a winning ticket, ninety-seven thousand to be exact. Have a nice life Luigi!"

Bill walked away taking note of the store clerk's mouth which was wide open watching Bill with a look of complete shock.

"Nicely done John. The mattress truck was pure genius."

"I thought so. Looks like I'm getting the hang of this gig a little bit now Murphy. You know, I didn't realize that I get to do wacky stuff like this. When God asked me to save Bill Taggart I was pretty confused especially since you and the big guy took me out in such a comedy of errors kinda way. What gives? I mean, Bill was really fucking up big time.....how come he got to live and I'm up here doing this?"

"Everyone has a destiny John....Bill hasn't realized his yet but that was one hell of an epiphany he had tonight wouldn't you say?"

"Yeah, I guess so. So what is his destiny Murph?"

"Can't tell ya that John.....he still has free will."

"Interesting."

Destiny According To Louie

Louie wandered along with the rest of the group. His head wasn't in the march ahead but was instead, focused on the image of his friend Gerald. He just couldn't shake the thought of what might await him.

"Life just isn't fair." Louie thought as one of the lieutenants waved him back into the line.

"I didn't think he was all that bad for having the courage to be himself and make a decision on his own for a change, I mean why are we following these stupid rules anyway?"

"Psst....pssstt...Louie. Ya gotta pay attention dude or you're gonna get a thrashing.....you don't need that now do you?"

Louie's other friend, Tommy spoke in a hushed tone as they all continued the daily march.

"Why should I keep quiet Tom? Something isn't right with all this.....and I'm gettin' tired of keeping quiet and marching in a line everywhere! Why can't I *go* where *I* want....and do what *I* want....when *I* want to do it? Answer that one for me Tom."

"Sshhhhh Louie........I don't want any trouble with the elder council......and I don't want to go to hell either....so just straighten up OK...."

"Tom, you are the biggest wussy of all time! The elders just preach about hell to scare us. It's all a tool for control man! What kind of God would condemn any good crustacean to boiling water and fire! Tell me Tom, I mean that would make God more brutal than us and he is supposed to be all knowing, wise and eternally compassionate......how can violence and suffering even be a part of his plan?"

"I don't know Louie but I don't wanna find out, you just gotta give it over to him and have faith...just like the elders say."

"OK Tom, what about Gerald? He chowed down on delicious herring to his hearts content and is probably living in the light of the *top world* enjoying bounties aplenty right at this very moment! Meanwhile, we continue to march single file...picking up whatever scraps we can just to be a number to the elders...all the while dealing with a belly that is unsatisfied! Explain that to me mister, 'go with the crowd guy!' It's just not fair!"

"Like the elders say Louie, life is not fair but we all have a purpose and are fulfilling it just as they have laid it out for us. Why can't you just be content like the rest of us and accept your life for what it is?"

"So you don't mind this life we have then? You get off on marching in a straight line or should I say....herded. *Don't eat this, don't do that, you will breed now, this is bad and this is good.* I mean we all know right from wrong right? We're smart enough to know right from wrong..... right Tommy? I mean, it's that simple, if we all get along and do what we need to do to help each other, all the while doing the things that make us happy we can't go wrong right? Our kind should thrive. Right Tom?"

Tommy was staring straight ahead and saying, "la,la,la,la, I can't hear you."

"Fine Tommy, just keep that head buried in the sand.....but mark my words there is going to come a day when we *do* find out what's really on the other side!"

Louie and Tommy marched the rest of the day in silence but Louie couldn't stop thinking about what a tool for control this hell thing was and how the elders never had to do any of the work that the rest of them did....*and* were allowed to propagate at leisure.... they *always* had shelter from the elements of the ocean that threatened everyone else on a daily basis. Yup, something was very wrong with this picture....and Louie was gonna find out.

One week had passed before Louie finally got an appointment with the elders to plead his case. He had questions and wanted answers.

Louie walked into the cave past the two sentinels that guarded the elders.

"What is the purpose of this visit number 3725?"

The head elder spoke firmly at Louie.

Plucking up his courage, Louie straightened his claws.

"Well, first off. . . my *name* is Louie."

The elders looked on in silent indifference.

"I am not a number...neither are all your minions...and I believe that we deserve the right to freewill and being treated as individuals."

The head elder looked right through Louie.

"You do have the right to your own freewill. That has never been in dispute. However, we know what is best for you and are only trying to guide you down a healthy, happy path...away from temptation."

Louie was furious inside as he had heard this mantra his whole life.

"Then why can't we partake of the bounty in the cage?"

Louie was indignant.

A cloud of anger passed in front of the head elders eyes.

"Because young upstart, the cage leads to unimaginable suffering and death!"

The head elder was raising his voice now.

Louie faltered imperceptibly but he needed answers.

"But the cages are filled with food in abundance! Why do we have to march all over the place to find scraps of food when the cages are filled with delicious herring? I mean, it must be there for a reason right? You say that the temptation of the cage will lead to hell...but I say that God must have put it there for us to eat delicious food and then be taken to the light above!"

"The cage only brings suffering young one! Have you forgotten the teachings of the great and wise Shambanara! He saw where the cage leads to and only by the grace of God did he escape...but not before seeing his brothers and sisters boiled alive, screaming for mercy to the *top world* demons who eat us for their pleasure!"

"I'm just not buying it!"

Louie pounded his claws on the sandy bottom sending clouds of sand floating all around the council chamber.

The head elder now rose back on his tail and stared down at Louie.

"Well then...I believe we have reached an impasse. Number 3725, we have nothing left to discuss...now begone with you!"

Louie walked back to his small hole in the coral stewing in the sour juices of his meeting with the elders.

"I'll show them." He mumbled

"Hey Lou....pssst...Louie."

It was Tommy.

"How did the meeting go?"

"How do you think it went!"

"That bad huh."

"Yup."

Whatcha gonna do Lou?"

"I'm gonna show them all Tommy! I'm gonna show them all!"

"Oh no Lou, don't do anything rash now!"

"Don't worry Tommy, you just keep on following the herd."

Tommy watched Louie walk away and knew that nothing good could come from this turn of events.

Louie waited until the coral had gone quiet and the sentries started to get lackadaisical in their patrols and then made his move.

Skirting around the edge of the coral reef, he watched as the sentry passed by his hiding place and then in one short burst, Louie headed out toward the open ocean.

The next evening, Tommy lined up for the nighttime march as the lieutenants were taking roll call. There was still no sign of Louie. The lieutenant called out.

"3725!"

Tommy knew there would be no answer.

"3725!!"

The two lieutenants continued down the list without blinking, it was not their problem anymore, but rather something to be written down in a report for the elders to handle.

"Move out!"

And so the march began.

Tommy marched in line with the others and after half an hour he heard rumblings of "another one in the cage" and his heart sank. As he looked ahead, he could see a cage materialize from the gloom and shifting sand of the ocean floor. Drawing closer he saw Louie in the cage with a big smile.

"Tommy! Hey Tommy! You should try this man! All the herring you can eat!"

One of the lieutenants was immediately on the scene.

"Keep moving! He is not your concern!"

"But he is my friend."

"He has made his choice, now move!"

Tommy looked back at Louie who was waving a claw at him and smiling. He looked at the long line of lobsters ahead and behind him.

"Be an individual Tom! Not a number!" Louie continued waving.

Tommy hesitated for a second and then in the spur of the moment, he broke rank and raced toward the cage as the lieutenant gave chase.

101

"Come back! You are signing your death wish!"

But it was too late. Tommy was younger and quicker than the older lieutenant and before he knew it, Tommy was in the cage with Louie.

"You've signed your death warrant!" The lieutenant puffed in ragged breaths and headed back to the line shouting, "move out!"

Louie and Tommy watched the marching line of lobsters disappear into the haze of the ocean floor.

"Well buddy, you're gonna see that I'm right...here have some herring!"

Tommy ate the herring and it was so good that he soon found himself believing firmly that he had indeed made the right decision. The two lobsters ate their fill and just as they were reclining back on their tails to enjoy the digestion of the best meal they had ever had, the cage began to shake violently.

"Here we go Tommy! Now it's onward and upward!"

And with that, the cage rose from the ocean floor and headed rapidly toward the light above and the manifestation of their destiny according to Louie.

THE GOLF GAME

Ryan Kemper hated the second weekend in July. Every year since graduating from college, he and two of his best friends would meet at Pebble beach golf course in northern California and spend the whole weekend reminiscing, partying and golfing. Ryan loved everything but the golfing as he quite frankly, stunk.

Despite practicing any chance he got, he never improved at the game and his frustration grew, culminating in ridicule and taunting at the merciless hands of his friends every July. Now on a slightly chilly, hazy morning Ryan and his buddies stood at the tee-off to the first hole at Pebble beach and the taunting had already begun.

"Hey Ryan! The hole is that way!" It was Gus Bradford who started the jabs this year.

"Yeah, well are you talking about golf or the other hole that Ryan could never seem to find?" Terry Hanson quipped with a wry grin.

"Yeah, yeah, yeah......you guys are about as funny as anal leakage." Ryan was already frustrated.

"Whadda ya think Terry, should we let Ryan go first so we can go get a beer while he finds his way out of the woods after he slices it to the right?"

"Very funny Gus." Ryan put his ball on the tee.

"Nah, I have a feeling he is gonna beat us this year Gus....."

Terry and Gus laughed and high fived at this remark.

Ryan cozied up to the ball and drew back.

"Quiet Gus. Here goes the ace."

Ryan swung the club with all his might.

THWACK!

"Ooohh.....now that's a slice Terry......going....going...gone! Someone get the chainsaw!"

Ryan was furious as he watched the ball sail perfectly into the thick wooded area to the right.

Gus and Terry just laughed.

Ryan jammed the driver into his bag and slung it over his shoulder, waiting for the other two to hit their balls so he could march into the woods, find his ball and get this game over with.

As always, Gus and Terry hit straight and true down the middle of the fairway.

"See ya bud!" And with that, the pair hopped in the golf cart and drove off up the course as Ryan headed angrily toward the trees muttering to himself.

"Why do I do this every year.....it just makes me miserable.......this sucks."

Ryan was in the thick of the trees now and ripped his pants on a fallen branch.

"Perfect.....just perfect.....man, I would do anything to beat those two morons!"

"Really?"

Ryan stopped short and looked around.

"Up here."

Ryan looked up in the tree to his left toward the sound of the voice and saw a tiny witch standing on a branch.

"What the....."

"I'm here to grant your wish."

"What?"

"Your wish...you know regarding those two morons."

Ryan just stared and thought that he must be losing his mind as this little creature looked exactly like the "wicked witch of the west"

104

from the *Wizard of Oz*.....except this one was only about two feet high.

"You can't be real. . ." Ryan stammered.

"Oh I'm real all right but I don't have all day so do you want me to help you or not?"

Ryan paused.

"Hello? Anyone home?"

"Yeah I'm here..." Ryan thought quickly and decided he had nothing to lose.

"Then what's your wish young man?"

"I want to be the best golfer.....ever....."

"That would fix those two morons all right. Now are you sure that's what you want?"

"Yes, I'm sure."

"OK but I must tell you that if I grant this wish, there is a side effect that will happen to you which I cannot reveal. That said, do you still want to be the best golfer ever?"

"Yes, no doubt about it!"

And with that the witch produced a tiny wand, waved it at Ryan and said, "let it be so!" and disappeared.

Ryan stood perplexed and wondered what just happened but as he looked down he spotted his errant ball.

"Well, let's see if this works."

Ryan pulled out his 7 iron and swung at the ball.

THWAP!

The ball flew out of he woods and headed down the fairway landing on the green.

Ryan walked to the green with a smile and saw Gus and Terry's shocked faces.

"Man, that was a hell of a shot there Ryan." Terry was obviously stunned.

"There's more where that came from fellas."

For the rest of that game and the next three years, Ryan went on to not only trounce his friends but became unbeatable in any round of golf he played. So as Ryan sat on the plane from Phoenix to Monterey he smiled knowing that Terry and Gus were now the ones who dreaded the second week of July. As the trio teed up on the first hole at Pebble beach, Gus and Terry were quiet and reserved, only talking about things that didn't pertain to golf.

"Well boys, should I go first?" Ryan was loving this.

"Yeah, like it matters.....you're gonna smoke us again Ryan......I'd just assune get a beer and hang out." Gus looked down at the turf as he spoke.

Ryan just smiled and teed up his ball.

Aw c'mon guys....it's just for fun right? Besides, I took a lot of crap from you two for a long time."

"Just hit the ball Ryan so me and Gus can get to drinkin'."

Ryan squared up with the ball and wondered if that little witch was still in those woods....after all he wanted to thank her.

THWACK!

The ball sliced into the woods to the right with Gus and Terry following the balls progress mouths agape.

"Well, guess I better go get my ball." And with that, Ryan marched off into the woods.

Ryan headed toward the tree where the witch was four years ago and sure enough.....there she was again.

"Well hello there young man. How is everything working out for you?"

"Fantastic! I am unbeatable on the golf course! I am so happy....I can't thank you enough!"

"Okay but....what about the side effect?"

"That's the great thing, I haven't experienced any side effect at all."

"Really......what about your sex life?"

"It's been awesome!"

"Really.........how many times have you had sex in the last four years?"

"Ummmm....let's see....probably around twenty or thirty times, give or take..."

"And that's good for you?"

"Man witchy poo....let me tell you.....that's FANTASTIC for a priest from a small parish!"

Destiny According To Louie
Part 2

"Hey Louie....pssst....Louie....wake up...."

Tommy kept nudging him with his claw but Louie was still out cold from the long drop out of the cage and into the holding tank on the boat. Tommy was scared and it was becoming a futile task to keep the other lobsters from crawling over his unconscious friend. More and more lobsters continued to rain down into the dark holding tank as the men above unloaded cage after cage of his ocean brethren.

"Hey punk! Get outta my way!"

A large fearsome lobster with holes burnt through places in his shell and only one eye knocked Tommy backwards.

"Hey watch out!" Tommy was scared but in no mood to take abuse from anyone at this point. After all, he felt that their common enemy was the men up on the deck of the boat and this was no time for fighting amongst themselves.

"T..t..t...Tommy....is that you?"

Louie was slowly struggling to get to his feet and was shaking off the grogginess.

"Oh Louie! Thank God....I thought you were a goner!"

"Where are we? Is this heaven?"

"Quite the contrary....I think we must have taken a wrong turn somewhere along the way.....starting with going in the cage....."

Tommy cast his eyes down and would not look Louie in the eyes.

"Don't worry Tommy...it will get better you'll see!"

The Socialite

"Nice tits!"

Skeeter Chilton sauntered past Audrey Newberg and relished the dropping of her jaw at his comment.

He always had a talent for saying the right thing to the ladies ...this he knew.

Skeeter had five hundred million dollars to his name after winning the lottery and making some lucky investments, the latest of which was an eight million dollar home on 17 mile drive in Pebble Beach, California.

Being from the Appalachian mountains in West Virginia, Skeeter loved the thought of living right by the ocean. According to his cousin Dustin, Pebble Beach was where all the rich folks lived near the ocean and Skeeter was now a "rich folk" so the logical choice was Pebble Beach. Besides, Skeeter always wanted to learn to play golf and he had enough money to take lessons from Tiger Woods if he wanted to.

Skeeter walked across the foyer of the mansion, through the crowd of wealthy socialites, trophy wives, 60 year old women trying to look like they're 20, and waiters with trays of hors d'oeuvres.

"Skeeter my boy, do come and meet the Dunston's."

One of Pebble Beaches wealthiest, Jarvis Weathermeyer waved Skeeter toward him.

"Skeeter, this is James and Shelly Dunston."

"Nice to meet you Mr. er...Skeeter."

James shook Skeeter's hand.

"Small hands equals small cock! Am I wrong there Shelly!" Skeeter winked at Shelly.

Jarvis and Skeeter laughed as James scowled and Shelly tried to hold back a wry grin.

Skeeter was fitting in just fine...he could tell.

As Skeeter left the trio he saw the old widow, Janice McGillicutty wave to him from out on the balcony and he headed in her direction. Grabbing a crab roll and a glass of Dom Perignon off a tray as he crossed the room, he reflected on how much he enjoyed being part of the upper crust.

"Helloooo....my dahling.....how is my young stud doing tonight? Are you enjoying yourself...or can I help you to enjoy yourself a little more...."

Janice cooed the words and made sure she let the breeze on the balcony open the slit in her ruby red gown showing off her beef jerky, lifetime of over tanning legs.

"Not bad gams for a 64-year old....wouldn't you say Skeeter?"

"Judging by how dry and withered you are from so much sun damage, I'd say that your vagina is the only place that might have any moisture left...and your face...it looks like a purse."

Skeeter could tell by the look on her face that he was on fire tonight with the witty banter.

"Cheers ma lady!"

Skeeter toasted to her with his glass of Dom Perignon and continued on through the party.

Winding his way down a marble staircase, Skeeter needed to pee really bad so he opened the nearest door at the base of the stairs. A blast of heat assaulted Skeeter as he walked into the kitchen where cooks, busboys, waiters and waitresses hurried about...occasionally yelling at each other when something was not prepared correctly or

110

fast enough. Looking around, Skeeter saw a tank filled to the brim with lobsters and a surly, heavyset Hispanic man tossing them one by one into a huge pot of boiling water. The five glasses of champagne along with three bourbons gave him an idea...he was going to release one of these critters back into the ocean as his good deed for the day. Skeeter marched up to the tank, reached in and grabbed one of the lobsters.

"Aye cabron!" Shouted the Hispanic man.

"Aye this Paco!"

Skeeter gave the man the finger as he turned and walked out of the kitchen with the lobster thrashing around in his hand.

Once outside, Skeeter headed out to the back lawn that was perfectly manicured right up to the edge of the cliff that the mansion was perched on overlooking the rugged Northern California coastline. The waves crashed on the rocks below as Skeeter sauntered up to a group of people who were looking and pointing at some sea lions sunning themselves on the rocks below.

"Whatchy'all lookin' at?"

"Hello....Skeeter...umm, there are some lovely sea lions down there...see." Katherine Jones pointed to the animals as the rest of the group braced themselves for the horribly inappropriate, yet always entertaining comment that was sure to issue forth from Skeeter's tobacco stained mouth...and the fact that he held a live lobster surely had to mean that this was going to be a doozy.

"Interesting. Katherine, will you please release this little lobster back to the sea from whence he came...I have other affairs to attend to."

And with that, Skeeter gave the crustacean to Katherine, turned and left the group.

Tony Perkins turned to address the others.

"That was odd...I was not expecting that."

"Yeah, that was way too normal for Skeeter...maybe he is starting to come around to a more civilized way of thinking." Katherine shrugged her shoulders keeping the still struggling lobster at arms length.

"Katherine, do get rid of that lobster." Tony curled his lip in disgust. Katherine walked toward the edge of the cliff and hurled the lobster out into the ocean far below.

Suddenly Marie Laport squealed.

"There he is! Down there, chasing that sea lion!"

The group stared in awe as they saw a naked Skeeter splashing through the shallow surf toward the sea lions on the rocks and getting close to one of them that was still sleeping.

"What the hell is he doing?" Tony felt his chest tighten...this did not bode well for the sea lion...that he was sure of.

In a final lunge, Skeeter caught the animal and a collective gasp came from the group watching the scene below.

Skeeter looked up to see all eyes on him from the cliff above and he just knew that this would make him a legend in Pebble Beach just like it did when he caught that sheep back home...of this he was sure.

Destiny According To Louie
Part 3

Louie reflected on what had brought him to this place. He had seen three dozen or more of his brethren thrown into boiling water and he was sure that he wasn't long for this life. How could he have been so wrong...why had God abandoned them to this morbid end? Tommy hadn't spoken to him since they ended up off the boat and into this tank and now Tommy had been pushed by the other bigger lobsters to the far end of the tank away from Louie. The creature that relentlessly kept reaching into the tank and throwing each lobster to his doom put his hand back in the tank and after fishing around, grabbed Tommy.

"Nooo! Tommy I'm so sorry!"

Louie tried to get to Tommy but it was over so fast... and then his friend was gone.

In that instant, Louie lost all hope and faith in God and a wave of such bitterness and rage washed over him that his vision blurred and he felt dizzy.

Suddenly, another creature reached into the tank and grabbed Louie. He thrashed around but it was futile. The sun blinded him as the creature took him outside. Louie was then passed to another creature who appeared to be the female of this evil species and he stopped struggling...he was doomed for sure, it was just a matter of time now. Louie quietly cursed his God for all that had befallen him, Tommy and all the others when a curious thing happened...The female creature hurled him. . . he was flying through the air and splashed back into the ocean.

The ocean.

His home.

He was free.

As Louie sank to the bottom he wondered what had just happened. Had God saved him? Why him and not Tommy....or the others? His legs touched the sandy bottom and Louie ran as fast as he could back home.

"That's quite a story Louie." The elders looked at him with accusing eyes.

"I feel so bad about everything that has happened..." Louie trailed off and cast his eyes down.

"We warned you, did we not?" The head elder said this so matter of fact and with no emotion.

"I know but...I just...well...I just couldn't believe that...you know...God could do that...and why was I allowed to live and the others...Tommy..." Louie wept.

The head elder came down off his rock and looked Louie straight in the eyes.

"Louie, be happy with what you have. Live in the here and now."

"But I want to have a purpose...I want to make a difference." Louie stammered as he spoke.

"Maybe your purpose is to survive the hell that you did so you can warn others about the dangers that lie all around us and especially the danger above...that's quite noble isn't it?"

Louie pondered this for a moment and then realized that the elder was right.

"Now go Louie and enjoy the life that has been given back to you and know that you can help others who would stray from the life that we have all been given."

Louie looked at the elder.
"I will."

Screwing with people isn't all it's cracked up to be

John Smith and Murphy sat atop the Great Pyramid as the sun was setting over the Egyptian desert in a blast of orange and purple that orgasmed together into a blood red climax.

"This is the best part of the gig John, you can be almost everywhere at once and see all the stuff you thought about on earth but couldn't do. I mean, look at that sunset . . . truly amazing huh? Reminds me of back in the day when I first got this job...in fact, we are siting on top of Pharaoh Khufu's tomb. . . boy did I give him a hard time...all the locusts and such...yup, those were the days! Now there are so many people that it is getting harder and harder to keep up!"

"I was wondering about that Murph...I mean, this is a big responsibility and I have to be honest...I'm starting to feel a bit of the guilt thing creeping in here and there...geez, people have enough in their lives to worry about without me making things even more stressful..."

"Don't worry young grasshopper...this too will pass."

"Yeah, but how am I going to keep up with all this after you retire?"

Murphy gazed out over the desert and did not respond.

"Hey Murph, did you hear what I said?"

"I heard ya...let's just say that what you do is all woven into the greater tapestry of the universe and you have to believe that everything will all work out in the end OK?"

John looked down at the slope of the pyramid and went silent.

"Hey lighten up there Johnny boy! You're gonna do great!"

116

"Yeah...whatever...it's all so overwhelming...you know."

"That's where you have to get a bit creative. Check it out, back in the days of the Pharaoh's and the Romans and such, there were a lot less people and it was a pretty easy gig for me. As the population grew, I had to figure out ways to get more accomplished with less energy so I had to invent things that would just mess with people and I didn't have to be there. Things that were a pain in the ass just by their very nature."

"Like what Murph?"

"Well, some of the highlights for me have been the invention of indoor plumbing, the internal combustion engine, and irritable bowel syndrome..but the one I am most proud of is the home computer and the *Windows* program! Talk about a double whammy! Let me just say that if you give the right person a 'bright idea' or invent the right microorganism , your work load can be cut in half!"

"Wow...that is unbelievable...I just always assumed that the windows program was created by the devil.."

"No, no, no that was little old me. And let me tell you something else, you think we have a tough job...you would *not* want Lucifer's gig! Talk about overworked! I used to see him once in a while at the staff meetings but for the last four hundred years or so he just sends his reports up to God via courier. I hear he is really stressed out! These humans sure keep him busy!"

"Well Murph, now that I am seriously depressed, how about we get back to work so I can at least get my mind onto something else."

"Sure kid."

Blood Is Thicker Than Dimensions

Jesse Livermore stared at his tormentors, slowly eyeing each one of them as his gaze moved around the poker table. He held the best hand...he knew it...but why would Bart Blackwell raise him only to have "One eyed" Jimmy raise again...Jesse smelled a rat. Looking down at his cards Jesse still held four kings...nothing had changed...except that if he called these two men and lost...he would lose his horse, "Cactus Jack"...and it was a long walk to Reno from Virginia City.

Jesse should have known better than to get mixed up in a poker game with a gunfighter and a brothel owner but he had one to many bourbons and felt bulletproof when he joined the game in the back room of the saloon.

"You gonna play poker or just sit there like a damned fool boy?" The brothel owner, aptly named "one-eyed Jimmy" after a dispute with one of his girls that ended with her spiked high heel shoe in his left eye startled Jesse out of his trance.

"I think the boy is yella Jimmy! Look, he's a shakin' in his boots!" Both men laughed and drank heartily from their glasses and the tinkling of the ice cubes along with both men's dead eye stare made Jesse's stomach turn over.

"Yeah, yeah...I'm thinkin' here fellas...."

"Well do something before I start gettin' impatient..." Bart leaned back in his chair and drew his Colt .45 from its holster and laid it on the table with a big smile of yellow and brown tobacco stained teeth.

Jesse felt the sweat start to bead up on his forehead right at the hairline. He was a trapped animal in this room with the two other men. He wanted to call the bet with his four kings but the smooth metal of the Colt .45 that lay on the table said he was beat. As he felt this eternity stretch into infinity, the room started to shimmer all around him. At first Jesse thought he was losing consciousness until both Bart and Jimmy started looking around mumbling and looking scared as the room they were in began to transform around them.

David Livermore lay in his bed at the Silver Queen hotel in Virginia City, took a deep breath and relaxed. Smiling to himself, he wondered if room 11 was indeed haunted by "Rosie" the ghost as the bartender and housekeeper had told him over a couple of beers at the downstairs bar.

He leaned over to the bedside table and grabbed his glass of Jim Beam. Taking a big swig of the amber courage, he felt the stress of the drive from Los Angeles and his new divorce start to melt away with every swallow. David relished the good buzz he was now feeling...it had been a long time since he felt so free and relaxed.

Suddenly, the room started to shimmer and get really cold. David rubbed his eyes but the room continued to look slightly out of focus. A growing sense of unease started to overcome him when out of the ether, a table with three rough looking cowboys playing cards appeared in his room. David was frozen in his bed as he stared at the three men who in turn, stared back at him...looking equally as surprised. One of the cowboys was moving his mouth and gesturing to the other two but David could not hear anything. It was at this point that he saw the roughest of the group reach for a revolver that was laying on the table and point it at the man across the table from him. . . . David closed his eyes and waited for the shot but it never came.

"What kinda 'Tom foolery' was that boy?"

Bart held the gun right between Jesse's eyes. The trio was now back in the saloon as if nothing had ever happened.

"I..I...don't know....I had nothing to do with that Bart...."

Jesse was stammering and the sweat was now rolling freely down his face.

"Bart, this kid's some kinda magician or somethin' I think we best let him go cuz I don't wanna have any trouble in my saloon....you get me?"

Bart smiled at Jesse and turned over his hand showing four aces.

"Could you have beaten that kid?"

Jesse swallowed hard and showed the four kings.

Bart laughed.

"Good for you that things went the way they did...or else you'da been walking to Reno! Looks like that fella in the bed was your savior on this day!"

And with that, Jesse Livermore got up and left the back room of the saloon, thanking his lucky stars with each step he took.

David Livermore pulled his white Ford Explorer into the parking lot of Peg's diner on Sierra street in Reno after the short drive from Virginia City. He was meeting his friend Billy Turner for breakfast and Peg's had world famous ham and eggs that Billy insisted he try. David was tired and still freaked out by the incident at the Silver Queen. He was looking forward to taking a nap after breakfast in his room at the Peppermill hotel and casino. Walking into Peg's diner, David saw his friend Billy sitting at a table by the window waving to him.

"Hey Dave!"

"Billy, it's great to see ya."

The two shook hands and sat down.

"Man...it's been like...forever Dave, how ya been?"

"Hangin' in there...it's been a little rough since the divorce, but I have a good feeling about this move to Reno Bill."

"Cool man, hey you look tired . . . lumpy hotel mattress?"

"Nah, I had the strangest dream last night Bill...at least I think it's a dream...it was so real. I dreamed that I was relaxing, drinkin' whiskey when out of nowhere, this table appears in my hotel room with three cowboys playing poker. I could see them and they could see me. Then one of them pulls a gun off the table and points it at the guy across from him...they are talking but I can't hear them....then they just vanished. Dude, it was so real...and the funny thing is...I could *swear* that I was totally awake."

"Where were you staying?"

"The Silver Queen."

"Well Dave, they do say that it's a haunted hotel."

"Yeah, I guess that's a possibility..."

"It's a crazy universe out there Dave...hey, I wonder what happened to the dude that had the gun pointed at him?"

"I don't know, let's hope he made it out of there."

An Older Conversation

Harry and Ben sat on the veranda of the Sunnyvale retirement home in Macon, Georgia. Harry was 82 years old (but looked like he was 90) and of English decent. Ben was 90 (but looked like he was only 82) and of African decent. The pair didn't know each other before they came to the Sunnyvale home two years ago. Ben arrived in May and Harry in June. The two had hit it off immediately. Every afternoon they sat in their wheelchairs on the western veranda of the home and solved all the world's problems as the sun set over the weeping willows that surrounded the Sunnyvale home.

"Beautiful evening eh Harry?"

"Yup, sure is."

"What do you value most in your life Harry?"

"Well Ben...I think that value is in a constant state of change for every man. When I was a kid, I really valued candy. Then as a teenager, I really valued any chance I got to be with a woman."

"I heard that Harry!"

"When I met and married my wife, I valued and cherished our love for each other. Then I got shipped off to Europe for the war and I really valued my buddies in the 82nd airborne and all our lives...when I got home to the States, I had a new perspective on the value of freedom. After my wife and I had our kids, that was all I valued...now I really value my adult diapers cuz without them....well, you wouldn't be sitting so close to me...lets just say that!"

Ben laughed.

"You sure are a crack up Harry!"

Harry looked around and leaning to the left, ripped off a fart just to drive the point home. Both men laughed hysterically.

"Ya know Harry, I'm 90 years old now (laughing) and that *never* gets old!"

"Nothin' like cuttin' the cheese to lighten the mood eh!"

The pair continued to chuckle and smile as they looked out over the veranda. Suddenly a hawk swooped down and snatched a squirrel from the lawn right in front of them and carried it off into the sky.

"Wow Ben, you don't see that every day!"

"Poor little guy never knew what hit him."

"Geez, what a way to go..."

The men fell silent and pondered the circle of life.

"So Ben, what do you think hurt really is?"

"Ya know Harry.....I think hurt is when you marry a white girl and your family can't stand the fact that she be white. Even though they are all smiles when she's around you know that deep down they hate her...and for no-good reason too..it's just cuz she's white...ya know? And then you go see her folks and they be hatin' me just cuz I'm black...and you can't fix it...you just can't...ya know...that's hurt..."

Ben stared at the floor.

"How can your own family hate the woman you love Harry....how can they do that?"

"I don't know Ben...I don't know..."

Harry and Ben stared out across the emerald green lawn that sprawled out underneath the veranda and out toward the trees when Harry spoke up.

"I think hurt is when you have an affair ...even though you love your wife...you know...shit happens."

"Amen brother Harry...shit do happen...uh huh!"

Harry's eyes filled with tears.

"And you don't expect to fall in love with the woman you had the affair with...now you...are in love...with two women....you're never the same man again Ben....never..."

"That happen when you were in World War 2 Harry?"

"Yup........"

"Did you ever see her again?"

"Nope...."

"That's tough my brother."

"You ain't kiddin'......."

Harry trailed off and Ben just stared at his friend.

"Time for your pill's gentlemen!"

Nurse Primrose (or, *Nurse Ratchet* as Harry and Ben affectionately called her) held the tray of pills and glasses of prune juice in front of the men with a big fake smile that was framed by too much makeup and a beehive hairdo.

The pair begrudgingly took their medication quickly so as to get nurse Ratchet away from them as quickly as possible. Nurse Primrose moved on to Ms. Wilson who was still knitting the same invisible shawl that occupied all her time. Ben and Harry both agreed she should have been put down two years ago...after all, the old broad was 102 years old and completely loopy. It was a grand source of amusement when she bit the newswoman who was here to interview her for her 100th birthday. ..Ben and Harry had a field day with that one.

"Okay Harry, what do you think constitutes a best friend?"

Harry paused.

"I think *best friends* are the people you know that would never judge you no matter what they knew about you...you are kindred spirits. They could crawl into the darkest pit of your soul and see all the

124

wreckage, shame, and fear that you harbor and still love you....because they see the true beauty of who you *really are* as a whole...good, bad and everything in-between. They know when to raise your spirits...they know when to leave you alone...when to talk and when to listen...they always say the right thing at the right time to bring you back from the edge...ya know...."

"Wow Harry, you sure can get heavy sometimes. I was just gonna say that it was someone who sticks with you through thick and thin...geez!"

"That's what I meant........I just tend to ramble on a bit after my medication..."

"Yeah, I know."

"Look at that sunset Ben.....I sure am gonna miss that when I leave this world......"

"Tell you what I'm gonna miss Harry....nurse Tyler's tits!"

"Oh yeah...and that caboose too!"

The two men laughed.

As if on cue, nurse Tyler rounded the corner and smiled at the two causing them both to straighten up in their wheelchairs and run their hands through their hair to make sure it was still as masculine as their aging libidos remembered...and not the wispy, unruly gray strands that now occupied the landscape above their bushy eyebrows.

"If I were a little bit younger nurse Tyler...." Ben winked.

"I do like my men mature Ben." Nurse Tyler blew Ben a kiss as she shimmied down the hallway.

Harry looked at Ben.

"You'd have a heart attack while she undid her blouse you old fart!"

"Yeah...but what a way to go Harry!"

The pair sat in silence again as each man tried desperately to imagine a situation in which nurse Tyler would have sex with them.

"Hey Ben."

"Yeah Harry?"

"When I was in high school I saw a young black man getting harassed by some white kids and I didn't say anything or try to stop them....even though I knew what they were doing was wrong...I've always felt bad that I didn't do something."

"Geez Harry, don't beat yourself up about that. You were young and it was the 40's."

"Yeah but evil prevails when good men do nothing...and I did nothing."

"So you're not Rosa Parks."

"No I'm not...here's to Rosa Parks!" Harry raised his glass of prune juice to the sky.

Ben followed suit. "To Rosa Parks!"

Nurse Primrose started down the hallway toward the two men to take them back to their rooms for bed.

"Well, here comes Ratchet.....always nice talking with you Ben."

"You too Harry."

"If I don't wake up tomorrow....well, you know..."

"Yeah, I know."

MEMORIES

Ronnie Evans was walking home, head bowed toward the horizontal rain from the latest in a long line of summer super storms that were making his hometown of Detroit the most miserable place on earth.

"What a drag.....this stupid.....constant....._fuuuucckkiinng_ rain...." Ronnie mumbled through clenched teeth as the small daggers of liquid kept pelting his entire body.

It had been 28 years since the polar ice caps had finally succumbed to global warming and lost roughly 75% of their mass, making places in Arizona, Nevada, Ohio and Kentucky very lucrative beachfront property.

Ronnie was only 27 years old so he wasn't around when everything hit the fan. His was always a world of suffering under the new world order (read- _super rich_) who stepped right into power after almost two thirds of the world's population perished from the oppressive heat, sudden monster tsunamis and famine. Now the remaining third that survived were kept on a tight leash. No gas powered vehicles, hair spray or other ozone depleting emissions. All luxuries were taken away and the remaining human population simply existed to survive under the "guidance" of the new world order. People worked at whatever job they showed an aptitude for and nobody got paid a wage as "big brother" took care of housing, food and transportation to and from your place of work. Only one child was permitted for government approved couples who were sterilized the same day as the child was born. People were either approved or disapproved at the age of 11 based on IQ and genetics and then sterilized accordingly.

Money did exist, but was now in the form of "credits" that were automatically sent to an individuals debit card. Everyone was given 100 credits each month for entertainment.

There was no local bar since alcohol was banned. Music and the arts were non existent now as censorship was rampant and strictly enforced.

"The abuse and indifference toward the earth's well being by past generations was caused in large part by their weakness in the face of alcohol, drugs and narcissism." This is what the high commander of the new world order preached from the head office in Nebraska. Diet was carefully regulated to genetically modified food that could be replicated en masse so everyone ate the same thing.....every day. The only entertainment people had was gathering together in groups to talk about how miserable their lives are and how nice things used to be.

One other constant was the V-chip or "obedience chip" as it was lovingly called by the population that was hard wired into everyone's brain. The V-chip was mandatory, without it you could not get food or water. You couldn't step out of line as your day to day events were transmitted to, monitored, and recorded by, the watchful eye in the sky.

As it turns out, Ronnie showed an aptitude with computers and quickly worked his way to the outer offices of the IT department that processed and compiled files for the government. He was also responsible for designing new chips and programs for various tasks the new world order deemed necessary.

Ronnie knew every move that the government made and how to get around it.........including the V-chip. Ronnie had re-wired his V-chip

128

so that it transmitted a separate signal showing him to be a model citizen.....even though he was doing things that he shouldn't. Essentially, Ronnie lived off the grid. Exploiting the V-chip was Ronnie's ticket out of Detroit to an island called H-4 in the pacific that was inconsequential enough to stay off the NWO's radar and had become a small paradise for those with enough credits, ten million to be exact, to make the journey with one of the rogue ships that ran such covert errands.

Ronnie finally saw his house appear through the torrential rain and grew excited at the prospect of being dry. Opening the door, he stepped into the entryway and out of the rain. Taking off his coat and hat, he turned to his left and saw three people tied to chairs in his small but accommodating living room. He slowly walked toward the three helpless individuals and took note of the terror in their teary eyes and heard the muffled cries from underneath the gags which were tightly tied around their mouths.

"Hey jerk off! Did you finish it? These three were awfully hard to round up and keep quiet! The lady bit me!"

Ronnie turned around to see his childhood friend, Tom Wagner looming behind him. Tom was an imposing man, six foot nine with wild staring eyes and a disposition to match. Tom had an aptitude for smashing things and was therefore sentenced to a life of back breaking work in the coal mines. Tom didn't understand how Ronnie built the chip but knew an opportunity when he saw one. It took Ronnie all of thirty-seven seconds to enlist Tom as the muscle in his plan and reprogram his V-chip so Tom was also off the grid.

"Yeah, I finished it.......this is gonna be big Tom.....I can feel it."

Ronnie pulled out a small metal box and slowly opened it to reveal a small palm pilot type device and three small micro chips, each the size of a grain of rice.

"This had better work Ronnie. Do you know how hard it was to get around the 'watchers' and kidnap these 'oldies'?"

"I know, I know.....you're the best Tom, that's why I hired you, now help me hook up the first one."

Tom looked toward the three hostages.

"Which one ya want first?"

"I dunno, how about the lady."

Tom walked over to her and picked her up, chair and all. In one quick motion of brute strength he put her in front of the other two men next to a table that had a laptop computer which housed the *Vampire* program.

"Why you call that thing the *Vampire* anyway?"

"Because Tom, it is going to suck the memories out of these fine folks who are old enough to remember the good times before the new world order. Then we will sell their memories to the highest bidder until we have enough credits to get on that fucking boat and get out of this miserable hell of an existence."

"You think people will really pay for someone else's memories Ronnie?"

"Hell yeah! Wouldn't you? I mean look around Tom. Everyone is miserable and just looking for something to brighten their darkness.....this is the new drug baby! And our ticket outa here!"

Ronnie knew how powerful any hope in this new age was and had developed his *Vampire* program over the last year in order to get on that boat to H-4 and live the rest of his days away from this misery. He tested the program on Tom and himself three weeks ago with great success. Using the wi-fi connection on his laptop he was able to access Tom's V-chip and see all of his memories on his computer in chronological order and clear as day. He then used *Vampire* to "suck out" Tom's memory of beating up a fellow miner and was able to send it to his own V-chip. Tom lost the memory and now Ronnie remembers the incident as if it were his own....clear as day and with all the intensity that Tom felt at the time of the actual confrontation.

Now Ronnie looked at the wild staring eyes of the bound and gagged old woman in front of him and heard the beep of his laptop as *Vampire* accessed her V-chip. Now he could see her memories start to play on the screen before him and watched her horrified and confused eyes as her life played out before them on the screen. Her first Christmas, baking cookies with her Mom, losing her virginity, first orgasm, and wedding. . . among thousands of others. Then came a trip to Hawaii with her husband, sailing on a catamaran while the sun set in a blinding display of orange and red above the turquoise ocean as the sails billowed while they toasted with champagne.
"That's a good one wouldn't you say Tom?"
"Yeah....sure is pretty and they are so happy. Someone will pay big for that."
Ronnie pressed a button on his keyboard and the old lady shuddered as he downloaded her memory into one of the three small chips.
All in all they downloaded eight memories from the lady. Horseback riding on the beach in Australia while splashing through the surf. Skiing in Aspen. Thanksgiving with her husband and all their children laughing together and toasting the closeness and health of their family. Of course the big payday was the births of all her four children. Since most people were sterilized and not allowed to procreate this would be worth big bucks to the right woman....especially in conjunction with the wonderful Thanksgiving and all that love and crap. Ronnie could almost smell the salt air of H-4. ·
"Next!"

The two old men looked completely horrified as Tom drug the old lady away from the table and started toward them.

"Who's next Ronnie?"

"Doesn't matter.....how about him."

The old man struggled wildly and his gag fell out of his mouth.

"No....no...please don't do this to me......it's all I have left......"

His eyes darted to the old lady who sat motionless. She was staring off into space looking at nothing but also looking as if something were very wrong with her soul.

"Jesus Tom put that gag back in."

"Please don't do this . . . I just lost my wife of 60 years to cancer....her memory is all I have left......"

"Shut up old man! You ain't long for this world anyway....besides, aren't you glad that you can make someone else happy?"

Ronnie laughed as Tom put the gag back and dragged the old man to the table and the waiting *Vampire*.

The old guy was right, he had a lot of great memories with his wife. They were high school sweethearts and Ronnie was able to extract their first kiss behind the bleachers at the junior prom, their passionate lovemaking and resulting three kids. The purchase of their first house and countless walks together, holding hands and being so in love. This was good stuff thought Ronnie...this guy used to be so happy....he was going to make him a lot of credits. Ronnie continued stealing the old man's life for five hours taking a total of seven hundred and sixty-two memories. Ronnie thought, this guy alone might be able to pay for the boat ride.

Tom dragged the old guy away from the *Vampire* and placed him next to the lady. Tears were streaming down the man's face, yet he looked confused as if he didn't know why he was crying.

"One more Tom, let's get on with this."

132

Tom dragged the last victim to the waiting *Vampire*.

This guy was as cool as a cucumber with a steeled gaze. He showed no fear and didn't struggle at all.

"That's the spirit, you old geezer. No need to be a baby like those other two. And just think, I'm such a considerate fellow that when I'm done with you I will hook all of you back up and erase the memory of all this so that when you go back to your pathetic lives, you won't know that you are missing anything."

The man just stared straight ahead as the familiar beep of the *Vampire* let Ronnie know it was ready to "feed".

As *Vampire* whirred and clicked, the screen before them was blank, there was nothing.

"What the?"

Ronnie was pissed, he only needed a couple more hours and he would be rolling in credits and well on his way out of here.

"What's wrong Ronnie, I don't see nothin'."

"I don't know Tom....wait here's something...."

The screen slowly faded from black to gray and then the face of a terrified woman appeared, hands outstretched in front of her, screaming bloody murder. Then the man leaned forward, bit her neck and blood sprayed everywhere. Ronnie and Tom looked on in horror as the same grisly scene appeared over and over again but with different people...some women, some men.

"What the fuck is this shit Ronnie?"

"Looks like this old guy is a serial killer psychopath or something!"

"Not exactly gentlemen."

Ronnie and Tom wheeled around to see the old man out of the chair with no gag and free of his bindings. Huge fangs dripped saliva as the man grinned from ear to ear.

"Now it's my turn to feed boys!"

A Happy Ending For George

George was completely spent. He had been struggling for the better part of forty-five minutes and the cold hard reality was now as clear as the water that held him prisoner. George had tried every technique the kayak instructor had taught him...to no avail.

Kayaking down the Snake River in Wyoming had been on his, *"things to do before I die"* list. As fate would have it, he was possibly looking at the end of the line...and his list if he could not break free of the hydraulic at the base of the rapid that now held him captive. With his energy gone and his entire body becoming numb from the cold water he sat immersed in, George closed his eyes and took a deep breath.

The day started so perfect for George, at 7:00 A.M. he was in the water with the instructor who showed him all the proper techniques that he would need to traverse this river...including how to release himself from the dangerous suction in the rapids. George was in amazing physical shape for a forty five year-old and being a surfer, he picked up on the feel of the squirrely kayak almost instantly. The instructors' reassurance that there was nothing on this stretch of river George couldn't handle set him at ease. George began his journey down the river at 8:30 A.M. with not a cloud in sight and the sky a turquoise blue with the slightest hint of a cool breeze that caressed his face and neck like a taunting lover's breath. George smiled and breathed in the cool, pure air as he paddled downstream on what he thought was going to be the perfect day.

George was startled out of his exhaustive trance by cold water washing him as the kayak flipped over. Now he was upside down and panicking. Splashing furiously with the paddle, he desperately fought the water that surrounded him. As he swallowed a mouthful of the liquid tormentor, time slowed down.

Suddenly, he was a child again, running toward his mothers open arms. Upon being swept up into her embrace, he felt the energy of her perfect and unending love for him. Then George was holding his daughter in his arms and felt the same overwhelming sensation. He then recalled a time when he was eleven and his father took him out into the woods on a back road and taught him how to drive. George was a quick learner and only popped the clutch twice. George recalled how proud his Dad was and could taste the soft serve ice cream cone that his father rewarded him with on the way home. Flash forward to the senior prom and the first time he ever made love to Sally in the back seat of the same car he learned to drive in. Sally and George were soul mates, he knew it and she knew it. Now he could see her crying at their front door as the police informed her of his death at the hands of the Snake River. This thought gave George a deep inner purpose and will to live. With all his strength he tried one more time to right the kayak. This time he popped back upright above the water spitting and coughing. As his head pounded, he got his bearings and realized that while he was now right side up...he was still trapped by the rapid...George knew his time was running out...he needed help...and he needed it now.

About a mile upstream from where George was clinging to life, Barry Silverman was fishing. He was still pissed off at his wife for making him late, "who starts a fight at 5:00 A.M.??" he kept mumbling under his breath... "Marjorie does...that's who...I don't ask for much...just fishing twice a month...and she still rides my ass...fuck me...it's not like I sit around all day watching soaps and Oprah for fuck's sake....."

Barry looked at his watch, 9:30 A.M. He cursed as he knew that all the fish were only really biting at dawn and he was way too late....at least he was away from her though. His pole bent and for a second he thought it was a bite but realized that his favorite lure was caught on a rock, he could see the glint of silver winking at him through the clear water about fifteen feet away.

"Dammit!!"

Barry pondered cutting the line but decided that he could wade out and retrieve it if he was careful. After the morning he had with Marjorie, he was *not* going to lose his favorite lure as well.

Wading out into the river, Barry expertly negotiated the rocks on the bottom and was soon waist deep, bending down retrieving the lure out from where it was caught.

"Gotcha!"

Barry beamed with satisfaction.

As he waded back toward shore, he saw Marjorie standing on the bank of the river, arms folded with a scowl on her face.

"What the fu......" Barry was incredulous.

"We have to talk right now Barry!" Marjorie was wagging a finger in the air as she yelled.

"I don't believe this..." Barry was stunned, pissed off and eternally tired all at once. As he grappled with all these emotions, he didn't see the slippery, mossy rock he so skillfully avoided on the way out. Instantly he was down in the water with a splash and floating downstream in the swift current toward the rapids, barley hearing Marjorie yell, "Don't you try to run mister! We *are* going to talk!"

George never knew what hit him, but it was big and it knocked him clear of the suction. Within seconds, George was two hundred yards down river and thanking God, his lucky stars and anyone else he could think of. All he could think about was his family and how he couldn't wait to get out of this kayak, drive home, and hug his wife and daughter.

Barry died an agonizing death at the hands of the same rapid that was denied George. As he floated out of his body and rose above the river he saw a lone kayaker heading downstream.

"That musta been what I hit.." thought Barry as he rushed faster and faster through the stars, planets and universe.

Barry ended up in a beautiful meadow where two men stood as if they were waiting for him.

"Hello Barry."

The man who addressed Barry was a normal looking guy but standing next to him was a balding man with thick rimmed glasses, paisley converse tennis shoes, blue tights with a big M on the front of his chest and a flowing red cape.

"Who are you guys? Where...am...I? Actually....you know what...I don't care...I'm away from *her*....is there any fishing 'round these parts?"

"Sure is Barry, right over that hill."

"Thanks...if you don't mind, I'll just be on my way."

"Take care Barry, God will be around in a bit to welcome you."

"Best news I've had all day! See you fellas later."

As Barry walked away from the duo, Murphy addressed John.

"And that my friend is one of my *greatest* time savers...came up with it a long, long, long time ago.....the nagging wife."

Murphy took a bow in front of John.

"I gotta hand it to ya Murph, brilliant work today...I am truly in awe..."

Stonehenge

And so it was on a sunny day that three year-old Promethius sat down on the beach awaiting his father's return. He could see the sails of the great vessel on the horizon at dawn and now the mighty ship was slowly making its way into the shelter of the bay. Running to the dock he smiled as his Dad waved to him from the bow of the ship. Promethius helped tie the ropes to the dock and the gangplank was lowered. His father strode down the ramp with a bulging sack of something over his right shoulder........a gift! Dad never returned from his travels without bringing his son something from a faraway land.

"Hello son!"

"Dad!"

Promethius ran to his father and hugged him fiercely.

"I trust you were good while I was away?"

Promethius tried to look at his Dad but could not take his eyes off the sack that his rested on his father's shoulder.

"I took care of everything around the farm Dad! Mom will tell you....I was really good!"

"Well I'm glad to hear that!"

The suspense was killing little Promethius and his Dad smiled as he knew he was, for all intent and purpose, torturing his son by not revealing the contents of the sack.

"I brought you something Promethius."

"Yippee! What is it Dad? I can't wait!"

Promethius' Dad poured the contents out on the ground. It was rocks of all different shapes and sizes.

"Wow Dad! I can build all kinds of stuff with these! Thanks!"

"Have fun son! Oh, you better take these out to the Salisbury plains where you won't disturb anyone OK."

"Sure Dad, thanks again! I'll build something really neat! You'll see!"

Promethius scooped up all the rocks, put them back in the sack and ran off to play.

The Hit man

So here I am again.......another coffee shop where the beehive hairdo is frozen in time on the waitress who was chewing gum as she took my order. I swear she was one unruly customer away from yelling "Kiss my grits!" She commented on the NASCAR T-shirt that I had on, remarking that I didn't seem the booze guzzling redneck NASCAR type. I just smiled and watched the sway of her hips as she walked away from my table.

She was right.....I wasn't the NASCAR T-shirt wearing type....I was more of a slick, whiskey on the rocks, suit wearing type. I was only wearing this stupid T-shirt and track suit pants cuz it was the only thing I could buy at the 24-hour mini mart after last nights job went bad and I ruined my best suit. God I hate it when they run and put up a fight......blood gets everywhere. I gotta buy a new suit......what a pain in the ass! It was getting harder and harder to do these jobs.....maybe I oughta just go back to straight, no frills hits.......I sipped at my coffee and thought about how I got here.

It all started with the good fortune of being born the son of a prostitute who would lock her child in the bathroom as she did her business......she thought it was funny to refer to my questions about my father's identity by saying only that his name was *John*. I didn't get the joke until I was about 11 years old. That was about the time I decided to begin straying from the nightly rounds of cheap motels and beatings that was my mother's world. The first time I stole food from a store I got away scot free......in fact, I never got caught.....ever......even today. I was like a shadow on law enforcement's radar. I've never been fingerprinted or gone to school. I didn't even have a birth certificate.....if I did.....it would be the matchbook from the *"Crazy Eight"* motel on Broadway.

When I finally got a hold of my first gun it felt so natural in my hand. At the age of sixteen, I knew what God had put me on this planet to do.......I would be a hit man...........but with a twist.....I would personally guarantee that I wouldn't just off the mark from the shadows but rather deliver any message that the client wanted to their face before I offed 'em. I musta been on to something cuz once the word got out on my personal deliveries, I began to get more work than I knew what to do with. Since I had no ties to mafia or any other group, I was the perfect man for any hit cuz I was un-traceable.

It was much more dangerous doing hits this way.....like last night......he ran away as I started to deliver the message and I had to shoot him in the leg to stop him and I hit the femoral artery so blood was spraying everywhere..... hence the track pants and NASCAR T-shirt......I had just enough time to look him in the eyes and deliver the message from the bookie who didn't get his money before his eyes glassed over and he was gone.

I've had some very strange requests over the years as most of my clientele were spouses caught cheating or had exorbitant life insurance policies. Business partners where someone was cooking the books were very common. The strangest request I ever had was from a middle-aged lady who lived in a wealthy neighborhood. She wanted me to off the pit bull next door who had used her Chihuahua as a chew toy. She also wanted to be at a safe distance while I looked the pit bull in the eyes and said....

"You're a bad dog for killing my little fluffy! Now that you're almost dead you don't act so tuffy!" Even the dog gave me a look of what I perceived to be humor at this ridiculous death poem spoken by a tough guy in a suit. Bottom of the barrel baby!

I don't care though...I really don't.....this is what God meant for me to do and I was the best. I would take on any contract as long as my fee was paid up front. Tonight's hit was a first in many ways......the contract came from a priest who insisted on meeting in the confessional booth. Just when I thought I'd done and seen it all....anyway, he wanted a nun named Sister Catherine taken care of as he claimed she was up to foul deeds within the convent walls and the only way to put an end to it was to take her out. I could tell by the tone in his voice that he was spurned by this Sister Catherine and his jealous ego couldn't take it anymore........especially since his personal message to her was,
"You could have had it all and more but you brought this on yourself."
Yeah....he wasn't foolin' anyone. I felt a little uncomfortable with the job ahead of me as it seemed that this priest was the one I should be coming after.....this was one for the books all right.....a nun for God's sake! For some reason I saw the pitbulls humorous look again within my mind's eye........except this time the dog actually laughed at me in this twisted visual. No matter, I didn't like the idea of killing a nun but reminded myself of what I do and after all the fee was a handsome one and paid in full. Besides, I was only doing what God put me here to do.

I left the coffee shop and went to my favorite suit store. After changing into my new threads I headed toward the convent as the last of the sunlight waned and the street lamps took over for the night. According to Father Thomas, Sister Catherine always took an evening walk alone so I planned to do the deed in the alley behind the convent that she used as a shortcut to the park. I took up a position behind a dumpster and lit a cigarette. This would be an easy gig tonight, I'll be back home by eight.

Eventually I heard the door open and out stepped the nun. She stood in the alley and looked up and breathed in the night air deeply. She slowly lowered her head and exhaled. With a broad smile she started down the alley toward the park and my hiding place. I stepped out from behind the trash bin with my gun drawn. She didn't look startled to see me and simply said,
"Hello there young man."
This broad was one tough customer......I've seen the toughest man break down in sobs as I leveled my gun at them....she just smiled.......wow.
"I have a message from Father Thomas."
"I know." She said...."He told me you would be here."
I just stared at her, this had never happened before....why would the priest tell her? Did she have a death wish....what the hell was going on?
"Sorry Sister, I'm just doing what God put me here to do."
She looked me right in the eye and said,
"As am I young man....as am I..."
BANG!!
My chest exploded with fire and I was hurtled down on the pavement! Blood was pouring from my chest and gurgling in my throat as I looked up to see Sister Catherine and Father Thomas looking down on me. The priest held a still smoking gun in his hand. My eyes felt heavy....I was going to die......
"How many hit men does that make Sister?"
"He's lucky number seven Father."
"We have more bad luck in this alley don't we Sister Catherine.......good thing I stepped out just in time to save you

143

again.....maybe you should try another way to the park......."
They both laughed.
I gathered my last breath and gurgled the word.
"Why?"
Sister Catherine looked down at me and said....
"Why silly, we're just doing God's work as well."

That's One Hairy Dude!!

Look at them down there......thinkin' they're so great with their four wheel drive trucks and high-powered rifles. Too bad they never figured out how to dimension shift....idiots! I wonder if I should startle them now or wait for night...hmmmm...the video always looks more spectacular in the daytime. I must pause to reflect on...ahem...*brag about* the one I starred in back in 1967 that Patterson shot. I was...and still am a celebrity...despite all the best efforts to prove it was a hoax! Ahhh, I was a lot younger then.:......I'm getting slower in my old age and this group of humans are the worst kind....red necks armed with rifles, beer, a video camera and a skewed sense of adventure. Let me tell you, just last week, a boy scout troop almost took out Gargamed and he is half my age! How was he supposed to know the scoutmaster and four boys in the troop were carrying guns! It never used to be like that in the good old days when you could just pass nearby their camp, let one or two of them see you and *wala*....the legend continues! No kids carrying guns back then, times were so innocent...yup, when the sun goes down it's show time...no sense in taking unnecessary risks.

You know, back in the day, you had to be very careful as the humans could use all their senses quite adeptly. You had to make sure you were upwind at all times and boy could they track....geez....those Navajos were the worst! Those hunting parties could track over rock! We were constantly having to slide between dimensions back then but now...well what with all the carcinogens in the air and ipods, cigarettes and any other number of technological sensory numbing devices, the humans have all but lost their ability to be in touch with the environment. They can't even tell when an earthquake is going to hit....it is to laugh! At least my kin have come to find a balance between technology and spirituality making for peace and fulfillment for all our kind. The secret is to realize that while technology can make things easier, it is also a relentless force that will continue to pull you farther from your own inner truth with its siren song. Staying true to one's core beliefs (never at the expense of others by the way) keeps us centered and empathetic to all that is around us. Once we figured out that enhancing dignity amongst all our kind seemed like the right thing to do....things just got better...that's just the way it is. Anyway, it's easier than you humans think, you just don't try is all......

The best part of listening to your inner spirit and being at peace is that it allows your brain to use more of it's full potential and suddenly new dimensions open up to you.....literally. On your present tack we figure you humans will figure this out...well....I'll be blunt...never. I guess that's not really fair of me...there are groups among you who are on the path but they are looked upon as crazy by the majority for looking inward and seeking information and not glued to the TV watching reruns of "Friends" and "I Love Lucy." I'll tell you one group we have to watch out for is the *Coast to Coast* crowd....now those guys are into all the wild stuff from UFO's and ESP to Vampires and Chupacabras to Bilderbergers and Masons! If only Art Bell and George Noory knew how close they are to the truth!

I digress. My apologies...although I have to say the Native Americans, especially the Shaman that used to roam these parts were on the right path until they were...ahem...forcibly thrown off the path...
"Whoa! Over there! It's bigfoot!"

146

BANG! BANG!

The shots bearly missed me and I felt the breeze as the bullets whizzed by my head. I was up with a start and began running through the trees with the redneck hunters in pursuit. Another bullet hit a tree near me sending splinters of wood into my thick fur. All my daydreaming almost got me killed...thank God for beer and the hillbilly's unsteady rifle arm! I could see that two of them had managed to circle around and get in front of me cutting off my escape route...boy it sucks getting old! I used to be able to deal with this situation so much more deftly when I was younger! Looks like I have no choice but to dimension shift out of this rapidly deteriorating situation...

THHZZMMPT!

"Where'd he go Billy Bob?"

"I dunno Jake, it was right there a second ago...he just vanished!"

"Look at the size of those footprints fellas! Man I told y'all this was a good area to find him!"

I was standing right next to the group as the conversation took place. You see, I was just halfway between my dimension and yours. In fact, you humans are surrounded constantly by inter-dimensional beings every day. . . except you don't know it. Well, to be fair you do know. It's the hair standing up on the back of your neck or the feeling that someone or *something* is in your bedroom late at night as you toss and turn in your bed. The shadow out of the corner of your eye... or the chill you feel on a hot summer day, that's us. The ghosts, the shadow people, the mothman, etc. And of course don't forget about me and my kind....maybe I'll see you out in the woods someday...

The Vacation

I had heard stories about the planet earth as long as I could remember. My father had visited twice when he was a boy and a teenager. He had fond memories of the third planet in the milky way galaxy. His tales used to entertain us for hours when we were little. That's why it's so exciting to be warping through the worm hole toward earth with my own family in tow. I sure missed my Mom & Dad but they had a long, happy life.....I mean.....one hundred and twenty-three thousand years is a long life span where I come from....especially now that they finally found a cure for the black hole plague.

Well as things go, the earth had not been so popular the last couple of thousand years as there were rumors of a virus that was starting to overrun the place. No one ever became ill upon their return from the planet but the rumors persisted......besides, no one wanted to visit earth ever since the new Aphrodite resort galaxy had opened. It was supposed to be incredible! There were planets for both adults and kids. My buddies told me that the adult planets had anything you could possibly desire or imagine.......whew..... some of the stories they told! Ever since the multi-dimensional personality splitter was invented, it was all the rave to have a guilt free experience as you could send the "bad you" to another dimension while the "good you" remained here and theoretically didn't do anything wrong.....my wife would never buy into that though!

Boy I tell ya, I sure needed some serious R&R and time with the family so it was with great anticipation that I now piloted our new family size star cruiser toward our destination. I was especially happy to finally put an end to my son's incessant cries of, "Are we there yet?" and eat something other than my wife's terrible cooking using the ships' rations. Besides, my Mom & Dad told us that the earth was one of the only planets that was in almost perfect balance with itself and the organisms that resided there. My mother had also passed down some great recipes for earth food that I was anxious to try.

Suddenly, the warning light flashed on the control panel and a high pitched siren let me know that we were about to exit the wormhole in 2 parla-secs and emerge about 10 zigo-sets away from the small moon that orbited the earth. I remember my mother complaining that she never quite got all the moon dust out of my father's star cruiser so we planned on skipping the moon and spending all our vacation on earth instead.

As we approached the planet from its dark side I noticed small pinpricks of light covering big areas of the planet surface. Suddenly, there was noise on my ship's transmitter and all kinds of alarms were going off as my ships sensors picked up artificially produced signals coming from the planet below. My wife and son ran into the cockpit demanding to know what all the commotion was about! I managed to quiet the alarms and start analyzing the data as I calmly assured them both that it was OK and they should prepare for landing as there was nothing to worry about. They exited the cockpit and I thought the computer had to be broken as I started to read the incoming data. There were extremely high levels of carbon monoxide in the atmosphere and a.......hole in the ozone layer.......and lots of metal objects flying around in orbit. I was puzzled as I pondered what could make a planet deteriorate so fast. There were no readings of a super nova nearby..... all the comet and asteroid residue showed that they never passed close enough to do this kind of damage.

I slowed the star ship to a halt......there were signs of technology all over the planet and transmissions coming from the metal objects in orbit........well I'll be..... intelligent life......this was quite a surprise! The odds against life developing on it's own in the universe is so....well... astronomical......and intelligent life at that! I couldn't wait to get down there! What a report I can bring back to my home world! I will be famous!

I pushed the steering rod forward and we began our decent toward the planet. I cloaked the ship so as not to be seen or detected by any devices they may have to track incoming objects from space. I was so excited! As we passed through the upper atmosphere I called to my family to join me as we flew closer to the surface. They didn't come. I called again and my wife slowly appeared in the entryway. Her face was ashen in color instead of it's usual bright purple.....and she looked terrified......all twenty of her eyes were filled with tears.

"What is it?" I asked.

She told me to stop the ship and come into the family area. I stopped our decent right above a pocket of huge thunder clouds. I remarked on how cool the lightning looked from our vantage point as it lit up the dark clouds. I walked into the family area and saw my wife and son watching our planet monitor. I stopped cold as I saw one of the transmissions from the planet playing on the screen. I had never seen such cruelty as one of the earth's beings cut the head off another being and others just stood by in robes and shouted loudly as if in triumph. What kind of beings would do this to their own kind? I quickly turned the monitor off and ordered my family to the rejuvenating area. My son whined in protest saying it wasn't his bedtime and he was scared of what he had witnessed. I sternly

150

pointed in the direction of the rejuvenation area and my wife calmly led him away. As they left, she gave me a look of sadness that only a parent knows when their offspring are subjected to bad things and a chink appears in the armor of youthful innocence.

I turned the monitor back on and sat down to watch and study this "*intelligent*" society. I watched through the night and saw images of war, death, rape, thievery, ruthless disregard for the environment and each other....perversion of religion and spirituality.....there was suicide and drugs and constant oppression in every society.....some had so much while most had very little.....there was disease, famine, extinction.....oh the list goes on and on...........I had no more tears to cry at this blatant disregard for the beauty of life and the universe.....this once great oasis in space was dying at the hands of this new species! My parents were surely spinning in their grave!

Suddenly the ship rocked and pitched as an explosion shook the hull! I ran to the cockpit! In my haze of disbelief watching the images, I had forgotten that the ship would de-cloak after 10 parla-secs! I jumped into the pilot's chair just in time to see a craft fly by and another off to the side of the ship launch a fiery projectile at the star cruiser. I jerked the steering rod and the ship took off into orbit instantaneously! I kept the throttle at full and didn't slow down until I reached a large gaseous planet known as Jupiter. As the ship came to a stop, I sank back in my chair and sighed deeply. The rumors were true.....earth had been overrun by a virus. A bad one too. With holes in her ozone, steadily rising temperatures and the dominant species being so violent and quite "*unintelligent*"....I realized that this once beautiful planet would soon die.

I paused and reflected on this and my eyes filled again with tears. My wife and son peered around the doorway to the cockpit and asked what was going on. My son had a look in his eyes that was a

151

little more jaded than it had been mere parla-secs ago. I smiled and said,

"Change of plans.......I've decided that we are going to spend our vacation in the Aphrodite galaxy."

They both forced a smile and walked from the room. Heck, everyone goes on vacation to the Aphrodite galaxy.......there's no violence, hatred or any of the other "old sins" that our race once went through a mere five hundred million years ago. Right now that seems pretty good to me........heck.....maybe I can try the multi-dimensional splitter....................................

The Final Curtain

Sarah looked out over the ocean as the sun rose in the western sky. Her throat was dry from the bitter air that was slowly cooking her lungs. A single tear meandered down her cheek, stinging the fresh cut there. She cradled the head of a dead man in her lap and wondered how last night could've gone differently.

Fifteen years ago, the United States fell under complete marshal law. The *New World Order* party had risen to power eight years prior as the American people struggled under the burden of credit card debt, foreclosures and outsourcing. No more Republican and Democrat minutiae....just one all powerful, straight down the middle governmental body that also functioned as the be-all and end-all solution to Americas woes. Universal health care, a fair wage for everyone, open borders and a zero tolerance policy toward any and all terrorism. Whatever ailed you, the *New World Order* party had the solution. It seemed like a good idea at the time and the *New World Order* party swept the election in a landslide victory. In the eight years that followed, the *NWO* party kept the United States embattled somewhere in the world fighting for our freedom that was threatened by the ever present terrorist. Oil prices continued to rise and corporation juggernauts continued to crush the "little guy." After legalizing all drugs and taxing them, the *NWO* was able to build the military to all new dizzying levels of destruction but gas prices now topped out at fifteen dollars per gallon and unemployment was at a staggering sixty eight percent. Right before the end of the *NWO*'s second term, it was decided that the *NWO* had to stay in power as there were two wars and five police actions in progress and this administration was the only one that could follow through with all this and keep us safe. They also announced the government's new sponsorship from Verizon and Chase Manhattan Bank to make or lives better and continue the battle against those who were either "with us or against us." Nobody ever heard from the Republicans or Democrats again and voting was suspended until further notice as laid out in the patriot act part 57 subsection 10 b. As more and more freedom was taken away under the umbrella of terrorism, something happened.....as freedom eroded, so did the American spirit. One day the country awoke to find that they were broke, stressed out, and over medicated. They began to rise up against the government . . .

It started with the militia groups but after two housewives were shot and killed trying to plant a bomb inside the Capitol building, the *New World Order* sat up and took notice. Military units began showing up in the streets of towns all over the country as small bands of rebels used guerilla tactics to take out army convoys. The streets of small town America began to look like the streets of Bagdad and for the next two and a half years, the new American revolution raged on. It all came to a head when the largest of the rebel groups, "freedom crashers" took over the city of Chicago in one bold, perfectly executed assault to which the *NWO* responded with a nuclear blast, wiping out the whole city and any living creature within 100 miles.

Moments after the bomb went off, Russia, who had been watching us closely, decided now was the time to put an end to the capitalist pigs once and for all and ordered a full nuclear assault on the US. India saw an opportunity to be rid of Pakistan, Israel launched on Iran and America launched on everybody. World war 3started at 11:11 a.m. in Chicago and ended five hours and forty two minutes later.

154

In the ten years of nuclear winter following the global conflict, there were survivors struggling all over the planet. Once the dust settled, the temperature of the earth rose fifteen degree's world wide which caused horrendous weather patterns. Hurricanes occurred year round, tornados were now consistently F7 or above and the rain burned your skin. The poles shifted causing north to be south and east to be west and the average human life span was now seventeen years. But through all this, Sarah managed to find love for a brief moment on a cold, foggy night.

Eric was a refugee from Hawaii and managed to make it to what remained of California in a small wooden sailboat that he stole from a dock in Maui. The journey had taken six weeks and he was ill prepared, resulting in severe dehydration, sunburn and delirium. When he came ashore in what used to be Santa Monica, Eric crawled up the beach and passed out under the blanket of the heavy 2:00 a.m. fog.

Sarah stumbled erratically down the beach after smoking two hits of Oppenheimer which was the new "super weed" that was grown in the radioactive hills of Oregon. She was trippin' on all the mutant crabs that scuttled away from her as she walked. As the ocean breeze blew, Sarah raised her arms and looked toward the sky drawing deep breaths and smiling as the harsh acidity of the salt air assaulted her lungs. Most people ran around with gas masks and goggles, covered head to toe in clothing....but not Sarah. She always dressed in whatever she could steal and her wardrobe changed daily. She was merely another shadow that floated around the fringes of the rubble that was the "end times."

With eyes closed and arms outstretched, Sarah continued down the dark beach splitting the fog in front of her like a wraith. When Sarah tripped over Eric's body, she fell face first into the sand and cut her cheek on a piece of broken glass.

"Oowww........fuck.....what a buzz kill....."

Sitting up, Sarah stared at the body she tripped over and slowly wiped the blood from her cheek and neck. Dead bodies were everywhere these days and this one was no shock to Sarah.....just more of an inconvenience.

"Why'dja have to go and die in the middle of my beach jerk....." Sarah addressed the body as she brushed sand from her hair.

"I'm not dead.....yet......and thanks for your compassion........."

Sarah jumped back. This was the first dead body that ever talked back before.

"Ya fuckin' twat! You damn well scared me good!"

Eric struggled to turn his head to look at her and Sarah could see that he was not long for this world. The cracked face and lips were swollen and sunburnt and even in the darkness with light from a half moon, Sarah could see the flame extinguishing slowly behind his eyes. Might as well give the poor bugger some company while he cashes in she thought, it seemed like the right thing to do.....even in her current "state of mind."

In the "end times" all the doctors worked exclusively for the elite who were holed up in a bunker / biodome designed to keep everyone out, and the new Adam & Eve's in to procreate and rebuild humanity. As a result, there was no medical attention for the vast majority of the population and if you got hurt....you could die.....it was now that simple.

"You look pretty beat up." Sarah sat down on the sand next to Eric, crossed her legs and placed his head in her lap.

"Yup........the good news is that I'm off that fuckin' boat though...so today, as I see it.....was a win."

"You sure are Mr. positive.....what *does* it take for you to get pissed

156

off and depressed? Geeeezz."

"Well.....let's see......no sex in two years.....that bums me out pretty bad." Eric smiled.

"Aren't you the saucy one....lyin' there all busted up and shit.......and still thinking with your other head."

"It's what I do." Eric said very matter of fact.

"Yeah well I tend to think that the other head is what got us this lovely world we now have to suffer through."

Touche madam......and your name would be...."

"Sarah, you?"

"Eric"

"Well nice to meet you Mr. Eric."

"Just Eric will do nicely thanks......huurrummph!"

Eric had coughed up blood as he finished speaking.

"Nice, you know this beach is disgusting enough without you doing that.....yucky."

"Pretty gross huh. That started about three weeks ago and I'm only now getting used to it....."

"So Eric, what brings you to lovely California?"

"Hacckkuumph!"

More blood.

"Well, I heard that there was still room in Hollywood for actors who can play the part of a dying man on a beach.......I'm pretty convincing huh."

Sarah had conditioned herself to feel nothing as a means to survive in this harsh new reality but Eric tugged at her in a way she had never felt before.

"Yeah, you're pretty good all right. Hey, can you play the part of a man who pulls through against overwhelming odds and rides off into the sunset with his newfound gal?"

157

"Wow, now you're being saucy......how come you chicks always have to think with your heart?"

"It's what we do."

"Right.....so tell me Sarah....what color are your eyes?"

"Blue with green flakes around the edges."

"Sounds pretty."

Even by the low light of the moon, Sarah could see that Eric's eyes were a sickening gray but she asked anyway.

"What about your eyes?"

"I guess that by now they are probably some sickly shade of gray but they used to be hazel. Ya know.....I really appreciate your hangin' out and all but I can only see shadows now, my ears are ringing and I can feel another big clot of blood coming so if you wanna go, I understand."

"No....I...um....don't mind....it's just that....well...you shouldn't die alone....you know?"

"No, I don't know.....I've never died before. I don't know if it's better alone or with someone at your side but I'll let you know when it's all over....deal?"

"Deal."

Sarah's heart was breaking in two as Eric lay there smiling and making jokes while facing the final journey.

"Thanks Sarah"

"For what?"

"Loving me."

"What....."

"You know, loving me. Showing love to a stranger. This is the closest I've ever felt to anyone.....I've had friends and lovers who don't have the capacity for love that you have shown me in the last twenty-five minutes. I wish I could live..... just to get to know

158

you......Aacckkk! Aackkk!"

Blood went everywhere.

"Wow.....Sarah....that is impressive huh! Show me another man who can do that!"

Sarah laughed.

"Seriously......thank you."

"It's OK." Sarah whispered.

In that moment Sarah fell in love with this dying man and wished she had a lifetime to spend with him.

"Will you hold my hand?"

"Sure Eric."

"Everything is dark now......my ears have stopped ringing so that's good. That was really annoying the crap outa me I can tell you...Haacckk! Hhaaacck!"

"Hold on.......for me Eric....please.....I ...I.."

Eric's hand closed around hers, his back heaved in one final convulsion and then he went limp.

Sarah wondered about a human's capacity for love. Even in these, the most hellish of circumstances, and thought what a crying shame that God seems to have abandoned us in our most desperate hour. Sarah just held onto Eric and her feelings as the sun started to light the horizon.

Well, That's Just Perfect!!

Nuclear war......there goes my career.
Just when I had it all figured out too. Ain't that just perfectly *perfect*...I mean...I finally know who I am, what I need to do with my life and who I need to do it with. Geeezz...isn't that always the way?

Let me give you an example....OK here's a good one....I know for a fact that we can all get along. Seriously...we can. White, Black, Asian, Hispanic, Middle Eastern...it doesn't matter, we can do it. Don't believe me huh? Why is it that all these different races of human beings, when working together, can put a man on the moon? How about a heart transplant or brain surgery? Oh, and should I mention that any man and woman of *any* race can create another human being....put that in your pipe and smoke it. Pretty amazing stuff wouldn't you say...hell, some might call these things miracles...and we take them all for granted...especially the whole newborn human being thing....and that's the biggest miracle of them all!

Ahem, I must apologize....I'm dragging my soapbox back to the corner now. Not that it matters anyway...I mean bombs are dropping all over the planet and I have the good or bad fortune (depending on your perspective) of living in Tennant Creek, Australia. Never heard of it huh? Well count yourself amongst the rest of the planet there. Tennant Creek is just five miles west of nowhere and ten thousand miles north of anywhere...aahhh...Tennant Creek, where the beer is cold and the flies aplenty...put it this way, wherever the nukes are dropping, I'm at the furthest spot away from any of them...but I digress.

The Aussie outback is, in my humble opinion the most desolate, difficult, charred place on earth..er...well now it might be considered an oasis after the radiation has had its way with the planet. Oh the irony! I suppose the coming "nuclear winter" will be when us lot out here will be checking out, but until then...hang on, let me get my soapbox out again.

There, that's better. OK here's the 411 people. Who the fuck do we think we are destroying the planet like this? I mean really, hasn't war been so passe for like at least 1,000 years? I thought we would've figured out the religious war nonsense after the crusades but nooooo, we had to continue to oppress the masses so a guy like Hitler could rally desperation into the war machine that he did and we were off and running yet again....sad, so sad. They say that history repeats itself and we have proven that on an exquisite scale over and over...OK you get the point. Trouble is, with these nukes and the oncoming un-survivable nuclear winter, the fly in the ointment is that this chapter in history can't repeat itself can it? Oops! We are *no more* as a race....gone! I mean "ba da ba da ba da, that's all folks" humans are going extinct. Ta da! Bring on the next millennia of cockroaches led by Keith Richards! One thing us stupid humans *could* agree on over the past fifty years is that they are the only ones who will survive this ordeal!

We had so much potential...it really is a shame. We got a fair shake too, the dinosaurs were wiped out by a comet that they had no control over. And we call them dumb creatures...at least they had the good sense not to extinguish themselves! It does break my heart. You know, if there is no God and humans were just a universal fluke, it was our great responsibility to protect that with all we had, wouldn't you say? We should have all been working together to keep the species going since we were given such an amazing, once in a lifetime, ahem, once in a *universal lifetime fluke opportunity*...pity. Now the other side of the coin. If God (whoever you perceive that to be) did create all this and us...what a disappointment this whole fiasco is...shameful really.

I should mention at this point that my wife and I just had a baby girl four and a half months ago. The petty part of me thinks that I had to suffer through all of my wife's hormonal craziness for nine months....for what? Just to have a kid who is now condemned to a terrible death. That's just a defensive mechanism though because if I don't marginalize it, I'll flip out and I need to be strong for them right now...I look at my daughter...knowing she doesn't have a chance...and well...you know...it just sucks.

You're probably wondering what career I was referring to. Well, I had just been offered a job out on the coast of central Queensland working out at the great barrier reef. What would I be doing you may ask? As you may or may not know, the great barrier reef is dying due to....wanna guess? C'mon, this is a no-brainer....global warming! Yes we have done it again! We are such a talented race when it comes to treating our planet with respect. You see, the reef is suffering from *white syndrome* which is where the coral dies and bleaches out due to warming conditions that affect the corals symbiotic relationship with algae. Now why would this be a problem you ask? Well, the great barrier reef is the largest living organism on the planet and if it were to be decimated...well...it would be bad for the planet's biosphere and lead to major problems for us land

162

dwelling creatures in the oxygen department....well not to worry because we have pre-empted that disaster with our ingenious splitting of the atom and today's firestorm of nuclear holocaust. Anyway, I had figured out over many years of lab work how to save the reef and...had this pesky war not happened, I was due to leave in two weeks to implement my life saving reef cure. My family and I were going to finally live in a house right on the beach away from the stifling heat of the outback...again....what a drag huh....just when you think life is going your way...BAM! Murphy just steps in and screws you...or in this case, the whole planet! Well I say, "well done Murphy!"

High above...in the ether of the universe, John Smith, Murphy and God all looked down upon the blue marble that once was earth but was now aflame and covered in a brown haze.
"John looked at Murphy and said, "did you do this one?"
"Nope"
Murphy looked at John and said, "was this your doing?"
"No"
Both John and Murphy looked at God.
"Don't look at me fellas, this was done of their own free will that I gave them...it's a shame... I really thought they were going to figure it all out this time around.... you know...guess it's back to square one."
John crinkled his face.
"Okay God, what did you mean by 'this time'? You make it sound like this has happened before..."
God and Murphy laughed.
Murphy clapped his hand on John's back.

"Tell me Johnny boy, ya ever heard the saying that those who do not learn from history are doomed to repeat it?"
John looked down pensively.
"Yeah Murph....it's not that hard a concept..."
"Indeed John...indeed..."

Made in the USA